WILLIAM BUTLER YEATS, Irish poet, playwright, and statesman, was born near Dublin in 1865. Although his family moved to London when he was very young, his childhood vacations were spent in County Sligo, and the spirit of the Irish landscape deeply influenced his future work. His book of poetry, *The Wanderings of Oisin* (1889), shows his concern for his national folklore. At this time he was living in London and helped to found the Rhymers' Club. His autobiographies, *Reveries over Childhood and Youth* (1915) and *The Trembling of the Veil* (1922), were written later but cover his life up to the age of thirty. *The Countess Cathleen* (1892) was his first verse play, and a volume of tales, *The Celtic Twilight* (1893), was published a year later. With the help of Lady Gregory he established the Irish National Theatre in 1899. He became Director of the Abbey Theatre and held that position until his death, contributing many plays, in both prose and verse, to its repertory. His volumes of poetry appeared regularly; among these were *Wild Swans at Coole* (1917), *The Tower,* (1927), and *The Winding Stair* (1929). He became a senator of the Irish Free State in 1922. In 1923 he received the Nobel Prize for Literature. His philosophical work *A Vision* (1925) was his ultimate formulation of a personal system of world symbols. *Last Poems and Two Plays* (1939) was the culmination of his voluminous publication. He died in France in 1939.

the
celtic
twilight

AND A SELECTION OF
EARLY POEMS

by w.b. yeats

Introduction by WALTER STARKIE

A SIGNET CLASSIC
PUBLISHED BY THE NEW AMERICAN LIBRARY

INTRODUCTION AND NOTES COPYRIGHT © 1962 BY
THE NEW AMERICAN LIBRARY OF WORLD LITERATURE, INC.

*Published as a Signet Classic
By Arrangement with The Macmillan Company.*

First Printing, March, 1962

SIGNET TRADEMARK REG. U.S. PAT. OFF. AND FOREIGN COUNTRIES
REGISTERED TRADEMARK—MARCA REGISTRADA
HECHO EN CHICAGO, U.S.A.

*SIGNET CLASSICS are published by
The New American Library of World Literature, Inc.
501 Madison Avenue, New York 22, New York*

PRINTED IN THE UNITED STATES OF AMERICA

CONTENTS

THE POEMS

CONTENTS

INTRODUCTION

No poet ever strove with such unwearied energy as William Butler Yeats to harmonize the discordant elements in his mind and anticipate the judgement of posterity with a poetical canon which would defy the passage of time. Even as a young man of twenty-four one sentence echoed and re-echoed through his mind: "Hammer your thoughts into unity." For this reason he was forever revising past work. When friends would throw up their hands in horror and take him to task for mutilating his favorite play, *Shadowy Waters,* in successive versions, he would say doggedly, "It is myself I remake"; and again on another occasion when speaking of an edition of his poems: "This volume contains what is, I hope, the final text of the poems of my youth; and yet it may not be. . . . One is always cutting out the dead wood." In many cases the total or partial rewriting created new poems which became palimpsests in which the early spontaneous mood and language stand side by side with the later metaphysical style, thus producing double vision. As one critic graphically says, it is as if Picasso were to paint over *Les Saltimbanques* and attempt to shape his mournful acrobats into the exact clowns of his cubist paintings.[1]

The majority of the literary pundits have eulogized the later trend of his work, and scorned the early poems written

[1] F. Parkinson, *W. B. Yeats: Self-Critic.* Berkeley: University of California Press, 1951, p. 133.

in an outburst of genius by a dreamy, idealistic poet whose mind, like that of the young Goethe, was a glorious chaos of discordant tensions, but dominated by the compelling urge to sing like a minstrel. Hence the supreme rhetoric of *The Wanderings of Oisin*, which was a new note in English poetry of the eighties, and the medley of styles in *Crossways*, with its poems upon Indian themes, shepherds, and fauns, many of which were written before the poet was twenty years of age. For this reason we welcome the publication in this volume of those early unsophisticated poems, the highly significant occult section entitled *The Rose*, and *The Wind Among the Reeds*, linked with *The Celtic Twilight*, quite the most intimate and artless book the poet ever wrote.

Many of the contradictions in W. B. Yeats that puzzle his commentators may be explained by his Anglo-Irish heritage and background. His family on both sides belonged to the "Ascendancy," as it used to be called in Ireland. The Yeats family originally came from Yorkshire, but had been established for several centuries in Dublin. On his mother's side of the family, too, the Pollexfens were of English extraction and came from Cornwall. The poet's maternal grandfather, William Pollexfen, was a merchant and the owner of a line of cattle-boats plying between Sligo and London. A fierce-looking old man with the eye of the "Ancient Mariner," he alternately terrified and fascinated his impressionable grandson, who in after years took him as the model of his Learlike, passionate old men. The poet's mother fades into the Sligo background, and her silence is in contrast to the dominating and garrulous personality of his father, John B. Yeats, the portrait painter, who combined Pre-Raphaelite enthusiasm with positivism in religious matters. Yeats père preached for hours on end to his dreamy, self-centered eldest son a gospel of beauty devoid of religion. Willie confesses in the first volume of *Autobiographies* that all thoughts of religion were killed by Tyndall and Huxley, whose ideas his father had dinned into his head. In spite of the father-son conflict which soon arose, and was to become a major theme in Willie's poetry, the elder Yeats, even as late as 1921 (he was then eighty-two), still tried to shape his son's poetical career and was ready to attack any critics who did not agree that Willie's later poetry was at its best when it was welded to concrete facts. As his father's oppressive positivism made formal religion impossible, Willie turned to magic and the occult, and he discovered compensation for his father's insensitiveness in his eccentric astrologer uncle, George Pollexfen. The latter's servant, Mary Battle, who was gifted with second sight, possessed an inexhaustible wealth of tales about fairies, leprechauns, and ghosts with which to regale Master William at any hour of day or night. Thus Uncle George's little house at Rosses Point was the young poet's favorite refuge—

> ——a ghostly spot where
> The wave of moonlight glosses
> The dim gray sands with light,
> Far off by furthest Rosses.

Mary Battle became an indispensable medium, but after Willie and his uncle had practised their evocations, later in the same night she would have frantic nightmares peopled with wild men riding horses in twos and threes on the slopes of the mountains with their swords swinging.

W. B. Yeats looked upon Sligo, not Dublin, as his spiritual home, though he only went there during the vacations. Just beyond his dreamland of Lough Gill, with its woods and its islets, stood the great houses of the Sligo County families that were to influence his life: Lissadell of the Gore-Booths, Markree of the Coopers, Hazelwood of the Wynnes, Drumcliff village with its church and rook-delighting trees by the monastery founded by St. Columba. Near Sligo lived all the clan of Yeatses, Pollexfens, Middletons, and to the South were Mayo and Galway, where dwelt the half-legendary men who became the glamorous heroes of his youth. The "Big House" symbolized for Yeats the eighteenth century, the age of Grattan and Flood, and the early nineteenth century, when there were

> Great rooms where travelled men and children found
> Content or pay; a lost inheritor
> Where none has reigned that lacked a name and fame
> Or out of folly into folly came.

Yeats as a boy of fifteen had lived through the grim period of the land troubles in the early eighties, when the first breaches were made in the bastions of the Ascendancy, and the image of the ruin of the Big House would be one of the last to linger with the poet in old age, and upon it he would base the most poignant of all his plays, *Purgatory*. But with the Ascendancy was closely linked the peasantry of the West, who inspired the poet Yeats with their yearning, their drollery, their fanciful speech and rich folk-lore, which he gathers for us in his own random jottings in the diary which he so misleadingly labelled *The Celtic Twilight*.

The harsh realities of school life in London or Dublin must have been agonizing to Willie Yeats. At school in Hammersmith he was bullied by his classmates, and he became acutely aware of the loss of social position experienced by an Irish schoolboy at an English school. And when in 1881 John B. Yeats brought his family back to Dublin and Willie was sent to the High School in Harcourt Street, he was not much happier under Mr. Wilkins, the headmaster, who wrote very bad and pretentious verse himself, and used to make fun of Willie's poems, with the result that the boy was ragged by his school companions. Those trials strengthened the hard core in the poet's nature. He soon wore down his father's antagonism by his tenacity, and when the latter made plans for sending him to Trinity College, he refused, and prevailed upon his father to let him enter the Metropolitan School of Art in 1884. There he made friends with George Russell. In his autobiographical *Imaginations and Reveries,* George Russell—or AE, as he was always called—describes Yeats in those days as "darkly beautiful to look on; fiery and yet playful, and full of lovely elfin fancies," and the latter describes AE as "a wild young man who would come to school of a morning with a daisy-chain hung round his neck." Another friend, Charles Johnston, attracted Yeats to the study of theosophy, and a young Brahmin, Mohini Chatterjee, happened at the time to visit Dublin. Yeats, in a revelatory passage written at a later date, said: "He arrived with a little bag in his hand and *Marius the Epicurean* by Walter Pater in his pocket, and stayed with one of us, who gave him a plate of rice and an apple every day at two o'clock: and for a week and all day long he unfolded what seemed to be all wisdom. . . . Alcibiades fled from Socrates lest he might do nothing but listen to him all life long, and I am certain that we, seeking as youth will for some unknown deed and thought, all dreamed that but to listen to this man who threw the enchantment of power about simple and gentle things, and at least to think as he did, was the one thing worth doing and thinking, and that all action and all words that lead to action were a little vulgar, a little trivial. Ah, how many years it has taken me to awaken out of that dream!" [2]

The most vivid description of Yeats in his twenties is that given by his friend of those years, Katherine Tynan the poet: "Willie Yeats, at the time of our first meeting, was tall and lanky . . . beautiful to look at with his dark face, its touch of vivid colouring, the night-black hair, the eager dark eyes. At that time he was all dreams and all gentleness: certainly he had not a trace of bitterness when I first knew him, nor for long afterwards. He used to be very quiet in a corner doing some work of his own . . . he never had the remotest idea of taking care of himself. He could go all day without food unless someone remembered it for him, and in the same way would go on eating unless someone checked him." She stresses his loneliness and his "spooky" personality. "There was something almost pathetic about him. He was so gentle, so eager to do what one wanted, so patient when one drove him hither and thither. He was made happy by so little kindness."

Yeats, influenced by AE, Johnston, and Mohini Chatterjee, was becoming more deeply involved in the occult, and Katherine Tynan described a "séance" she attended in Dublin with the young poet: "The presences had communications to make and struggled to make them. Willie Yeats was banging his hand on the table as though he had a fit, muttering to himself. Presently the spirits were able to speak. There was someone in the room who was hindering them. By this time I had got in a few invocations of my own. There was a tremendous deal of rapping going on. The spirits were obviously annoyed. They were asked for an indication of who it was that was holding them back.

[2] W. B. Yeats, *Collected Works*. New York: The Macmillan Co., 1951, Vol. VII, p. 191.

They indicated me, and I was asked to withdraw, which I did cheerfully. The last thing I saw as the door opened to let me pass through was Willie Yeats banging his head on the table." [3]

Yeats at those "séances" longed to fall beneath the spell and become "disenthralled," but he could never lose his reasoning power and suspend his common sense in blind credulity.

When the Yeats family moved back to London in 1887, Willie became engrossed in MacGregor Mathers and the ten Sephiroth of the Cabala, representing the archetypal man Adam Qadmon the Protogonos—the cabalistic "tree of life" on which all things depend. This great tree paralleling the body of Adam, which united the Tree of Life into one single image, gave Yeats the image for his important poem, "The Two Trees," and symbols for his plays. Eventually, when dealing with magic, he came to believe that neither is the thing seen ever the vision, nor is the thing heard ever the message, for if mystery and magic became certain and wholly believed, there would no longer be any magic or mystery, and in his own eyes his Sibylline stature would diminish through that certainty.

It was the irony of fate that John B. Yeats, who had resolutely refused to give his son a religion, should now become alarmed at the latter's personal experiments in mysticism, spiritualism, and magic. When Willie's great friend John O'Leary, the old Fenian leader, informed him of his father's concern about his dabbling in mysticism and magic, the latter replied angrily: "If I had not made magic my constant study I could not have written a single line of my Blake book, nor would *Countess Kathleen* have ever come to exist. The mystical life is the centre of all that I do and all that I think and all that I write." [4]

Those London years were full of activity, for Yeats was finishing his long narrative poem *The Wanderings of Oisin* (1889), which, in the Definitive Edition of his works in later life, he moved from its conventional place in the "Narrative and Dramatic" section of his poems to the very

---

[3] Katherine Tynan, *Twenty-Five Years*. London: Smith, Elder & Co., 1913, pp. 208-209.
[4] Letter to Sturge-Moore, March 14, 1925.

beginning of the book, probably because that poem is a first statement of what he came in his old age to feel was the major theme of his entire work: the horror of old age that brings wisdom at the price of bodily decrepitude and death. The poem is a kind of *Odyssey*, which Willie's hero, William Morris, praised as being "his kind of poetry," though there is the world of difference between the rugged Viking spirit of the Norse Sigurd and the misty and ghostly atmosphere of the West of Ireland. The poem received very favourable criticism, and some compared it to *Endymion*, calling it richer in romantic sensuous beauty than the poem by the youthful Keats.

On January 30, 1889, new light came into the life of Yeats when Maud Gonne arrived at Bedford Park with an introduction from John O'Leary. From that moment she became for him Helen and Pallas Athena, and in his *Autobiographies* he writes lyrically of her luminous complexion, "like that of apple blossoms through which light falls, and I remember her standing that first day by a great heap of blossoms in the window." He was soon to discover that Maud Gonne was an Amazon as well as Helen, and, try as he would, he could never make himself a great enough nationalist to satisfy her revolutionary aspirations. He concentrated now upon Irish themes and joined her in public meetings, and became through the influence of O'Leary a member of the Irish Republican Brotherhood. We find him in 1891 in Dublin, where he met Maud Gonne, who had come over for Parnell's funeral, at which, according to some who were present, a star fell into the grave. In that year he proposed to her and was rejected. His melancholy mood appears in "The White Birds," where the drawn-out, Swinburnian rhythms accentuated the remote, fantastic beauty of the Danaan shore. The poet was evidently distracted by his beloved's harsh refusal, for he threatens her in four poems he wrote for her at that time: with tears in "The Sorrow of Love" ("and with you came the whole of the world's tears"); with old age in the lovely "When You Are Old," recreated from Ronsard's celebrated sonnet to Hélène de Surgères; with extinction in "The White Birds"; and with death itself in "A Dream of Death."

He was also at the time deeply interested in Florence

Farr, the actress, who seemed to embody his ideal of the art of verse-speaking. Miss Farr, however, was also a devotee of Ibsen, and the poet struggled hard to draw her away from the lure of Ibsenism, accusing her of wasting her talents upon *Rosmerholm* "with its odour of spilt poetry." So powerful was the impression that Yeats made upon the actress that she devoted herself to him and collaborated with him in his first experiments in speaking verse to music. Her playing of the psaltery with which she accompanied her recitations made him more reconciled to music. Florence Farr was important in Yeats's development as a dramatist, and in later years she would appear in the "crazy Jane" period as the image of woman in her fiftieth year who dreads the pitiless ravages of old age and fading beauty, but he would never forget how she had helped him in his efforts to release poetry from its slavery to music.

Yeats in his poem "To the Rose upon the Rood of Time" declared that the rose poems would sing of his hopeless love for Maud Gonne, the Rosicrucian and cabalistic rites he was practising under the aegis of the "Golden Dawn" of MacGregor Mathers, and the legends of pre-Christian Ireland. He identified the Rose as a compound of "Beauty and Peace," "Beauty and Wisdom," Shelley's Intellectual Beauty, and man's suffering. In later years he used to refer to Dante's conception of Heaven as a white rose with a yellow centre like the sun. He introduced his Rosicrucian theories by making the Rose the substitute for the lotus as the flower and blossoms on the Tree of Life. "Because the Rose, the flower sacred to the Virgin Mary, and the flower that Apuleius's adventurer ate when he was changed out of the ass's shape and received into the fellowship of Isis, is the Western Flower of Life, I have imagined it growing upon the Tree of Life."

He was now taken to task by his fellow-members of the Rhymers' Club for "obscurity," and by John O'Leary and Maud Gonne for not writing poetry that was sufficiently Irish. He immediately defended himself in "To Ireland in the Coming Times," in which he claims to be accounted a true brother of the company who sang to sweeten Ireland's wrong, ballad and story, rann and song. "Fergus and the Druid," "Cuchulain's Fight with the Sea," and *Oisin* would be his first contributions to his idea of creating a great myth which would symbolize Ireland's destiny. "Cuchulain's Fight with the Sea" he would dramatize later as *On Baile's Strand* (1903), the central drama of his five-play Cuchulain cycle, and he declared that the Irish hero's battle with the sea symbolized man's agony when, maddened by the strife in his own mind, he takes up arms against the sea itself, the image of destruction. Out of the Cuchulain theme, with its struggle of father against son, Yeats constructed a mask both for himself and for his nation, for he was convinced that every passionate man is, as it were, linked with another age, historical or imaginary, where alone he finds images that rouse his energy. Ireland's mask, he imagined, might resemble that which is most unlike the known Ireland of priest, merchant, and politician—

An Ireland
The poets have imagined, terrible and gay,

Cuchulain's Ireland, a land of reckless heroes, "for have not all races had their first unity from a mythology that marries them to rock and hill? We had in Ireland imaginative stories which the uneducated classes knew and even sang, and might we not make those stories current among the educated classes, rediscovering . . . the applied arts of literature," the association of literature, that is, with music, speech, and dance, and at last, it might be, so deepen the political passion of the nation that all, artist and poet, craftsman and day-labourer, would accept a common design.

Yeats believed that if he, as a representative poet of his country, put on this myth-founded mask of Ireland, a new nation might arise from the Hegelian tension of opposites; for nations, races, and individual men, he goes on to say, are unified by an image, or bundle of images, symbolical or evocative of the state of mind which is the most difficult to that man, race, or nation, because only the greatest obstacle that can be contemplated without despair rouses the will to full intensity. "I had seen," he continues, "Ireland in my own time turn from the bragging rhetoric and gregarious humour of O'Connell's generation and school, and offer herself to the solitary and proud Parnell as to her anti-self, buskin following hard on sock, and I had begun to hope, or to half-hope, that we might be the first in Europe to seek unity as deliberately as it had been sought by theologian, poet, sculptor, architect, from the eleventh to the thirteenth century."

The poet in his exile in London longed incessantly for the Sligo countryside, and he describes how the idea for his most popular poem "Innisfree" came to him one day when he stood, "very homesick," before a shop window and heard the sound of water trickling from a little fountain. As a pendant to that poem he wrote in 1891, under the pseudonym Ganconagh, his miniature novel *John Sherman*—so artless and amateurish a piece of work that it comes as a shock after the occult poems of the Rose, and we wonder what was his object in writing it with its mixture of shrewdness and naïveté, as though the young dreamer every now and then gave his readers a quizzical side-glance to watch the effect he was creating as he unfolded his tale. The charm of the novel lies in the description of Sherman's native town of Ballagh (Sligo), which reads like excerpts from the diary of an introspective schoolboy: "The town was dripping, but the rain was almost over. . . . It was the home of ducks, three or four had squeezed themselves under a gate, and were now splashing about in the gutter of the main street."

The Celtic Twilight, which was published in 1893, is in every way a contrast to all the other works of Yeats, and its general note is one of complete sincerity and simplicity. The title would lead us to expect the prevailing misty melancholy of the poems of these years, whereas it is full of freshness and early-morning sunshine, and might have been written in the open air. Occasionally, we catch a glimpse of the rarefied world of the Sacred Rose, but all around us we see the familiar scenes of the countryside near Sligo; we mix with the village folk and roam with them through the woods, and they tell us so many strange tales that we begin to see fairies lurking behind hawthorne bushes, and when darkness falls over the sand dunes at Rosses, we see ghosts flitting by the raths. The book is based upon a diary which Yeats carried with him on his rambles; he would jot down little sketches and tales he heard, many of which he afterwards turned into lyrics.

The Celtic Twilight gives us a far more intimate account of the poet than the more self-conscious autobiographical volume, *Reveries,* for here he is not trying to work his life into any preconceived pattern, and is content to exist and get his ear full as well as his eye full from life around him. At one moment he is absorbed by the little anecdote he is told by one of his rustic friends, at another some stray memory strikes him and he goes off at a tangent after it like a boy with a butterfly net. This little book has more earthiness about it than many of the others.

Many of the tales were told to the young poet by one Paddy Flynn, a little bright-eyed old man who lived in a leaky, one-room cabin in the village of Ballisodare. "The first time I saw him he was asleep under a hedge, smiling in his sleep." It is Paddy Flynn, not the poet, who sets the pace in the book.

These intimate sketches show the author's immense zest for life, and in every page we feel that he is jotting down new impressions of human beings he has met in his expeditions through the countryside and that he has forgotten all about his own age. His pleasure was to rove the hills, talking to half-mad and conscience-stricken persons, hoping to persuade them to deliver up the keeping of their troubles to him.

A sketch which he calls "Dust hath closed Helen's Eye" describes his visit to the old square castle of Ballylee in the barony of Kiltartan, in County Galway, of which he would one day, a quarter of a century later, become the owner, and where he would write some of his greatest mature poems in "The Tower." Even in 1893 he continually visited that ancient tower to listen to the farmer and the old miller who lived close by tell stories about Biddy Early, a "wise woman" from Clare who used to say: "There is a cure for all evil between the two mill wheels of Ballylee." From the old miller Yeats heard tales of Mary Hynes, whose legendary beauty (she had died sixty years before) was still celebrated around the turf fires, "for her skin was like dribbled snow and she had blushes in her cheeks." Mary Hynes, the local Helen, had inspired Raftery, the famous blind minstrel of the West. When the woman sang the poem in the Irish, Yeats noted that every word was audible and expressive, as the words in a song always were, before music grew too proud to be the garment of words. So the poet went from cabin to cabin, questioning the old people about Helen of Ballylee, and one old wrinkled hag told him that Mary Hynes was "taken," as the word is, by the *Sidhe*. Mary Hynes died young because the gods loved her, for the *Sidhe* are the gods, and it may be that the old saying, which we forget to understand literally, meant her manner of death in the old times.

What the young poet discovered was that these humble folk were many years nearer to the ancient Greek world that set beauty beside the fountain of things than our own men of learning.

To those of us who used to carry *The Celtic Twilight* on our youthful rambles in the West, it became a kind of talisman, initiating us into the mysteries of the countryside in Sligo, and the spell it cast over us was more powerful than that cast by any of the poems of the early collections, because it told us the secrets of the raths—such as that of Cashel Nore where the treasure of the O'Byrnes lies buried under a spell that cannot be broken until three of them have found it and died, and it made us listen expectantly to the *grainne oge,* the hedgehog that "grunts like a Christian in the enchanted woods," where there are also cats that have a language of their own and are dangerous to meddle with, as the people say they were once serpents, and if you annoyed them "they might claw or bite you in a way that would put poison in you, and that would be the serpent's tooth."

The poet in this book too has been able to convey by his lilting prose the excitement he felt when he walked with some old countryman at night and fell into what seemed to him to be the power of faery. The climax of the book comes in the description of Drumcliff and Rosses, when the poet's prose reads like the rann of a shanachie:

"Drumcliff" is a great place for omens. Before a prosperous fishing season a herring-barrel appears in the midst of a storm-cloud; and at a place called Columkille's Strand, a place of marsh and mire, an ancient boat, with St. Columba himself, comes floating in from sea on a moonlight night: a portent of a brave harvesting.

They have their dread portents too. Some few seasons ago a fisherman saw, far on the horizon, renowned Hy Brazel, where he who touches shall find no more labour or care, nor cynic laughter, but shall go walking about under shadiest boscage, and enjoy the conversation of Cuchullin and his heroes. A vision of Hy Brazel forebodes national troubles.

Drumcliff and Rosses are chokeful of ghosts. By bog, road, rath, hillside, sea-border, they gather in all shapes: headless women, men in armour, shadow hares, fire-tongued hounds, whistling seals, and so on. A whistling seal sank a ship the other day.

Yeats always returned in his rambles to Rosses and Drumcliff, for it was only there that he heard the stories of fairies and ghosts. A few miles northward he was wholly a stranger and could find nothing, and when he asked for stories of the fairies the people would answer: "They always mind their own affairs and I always mind mine." Only friendship or knowledge of his forebears and relations who had lived near Rosses and Drumcliff for many years would loosen cautious tongues.

Even in the years 1891-1893, when Yeats was a minstrel poet who gave free play to his genius and produced his "dazzling yet misty" spells unconsciously, we find a prophetic note, as though, like one gifted with second sight, he foresaw the successive stages through which he would pass as a poet. This note echoes and re-echoes through "The Man who Dreamed of Faeryland," a poem first published in *The National Observer* (Feb. 7, 1891):

> He stood among a crowd at Drumahair,
> His heart hung all upon a silken dress,
> And he had known at last some tenderness
> Before earth made of him her sleepy care;

He too would never find peace in love-making youth, money-making middle age, angry old age, or mouldering death, for he would always be lured away by occult symbols to the things of the spirit—as the poem says at the end, "The man has found no comfort in the grave." In 1892, when Yeats published the *Countess Kathleen,* he was drawn more and more towards the theatre, and though he saw himself primarily as a lyricist, he had the temperament of a dramatist, for he saw his own character as a battlefield of warring personalities. Hence the voluminous notes which he appends to *The Wind Among the Reeds* to guide his readers through the occult symbolism. Yeats during the nineties lived in an environment heavily saturated with the aestheticism of Walter Pater, upon whom he lays the chief responsibility for the general trend of the "Tragic Generation" of Oscar Wilde, Lionel Johnson, Dyson, and himself. Of the three main threads which ran through his life and thought—namely, aestheticism, nationalism, and occultism—it is the first which explains his development in those years when he became a close friend of Arthur Symons and went to Paris with him. Yeats's knowledge of the French poets was at a second hand, mostly through the medium of Arthur Symons, who not only was the foremost translator of the day but was also a friend of Mallarmé and the principal French poets. With Symons Yeats went to see a performance of *Axel* by Villiers de L'Isle Adam, which became at once, as he said, one of the "sacred books." Nevertheless, although the poet absorbed some of Mallarmé's doctrines of symbolism and made use of them in practice and decoration, he was diverted from France and the symbolists by the second thread of the three threads—nationalism—which had in 1896 begun to monopolize his thoughts. In that year, which Dr. Henn[5] considers the most fateful of all years for Yeats, the poet went to Ireland with Arthur Symons and visited Sligo and the Aran Islands, then untouched and unexploited. In Galway, he met Edward Martyn, the cousin of George Moore, a devotee of the theatre and eager to adapt Ibsenism to Irish national drama. From Martyn's Wagnerian castle, Tullyra, the poet went to Coole, the country seat of Lady Gregory, who was destined to be his Egeria. For twenty summers, from 1897 until he rebuilt his tower of Ballylee, Yeats was her guest at Coole Park, where he was lodged and fed and given the peace and leisure to write. In 1896, too, Yeats in Paris met a young Irish writer, a Trinity College graduate, John Mil-

[5] T. R. Henn, *Lonely Tower*. London: Methuen & Co., 1950.

lington Synge, who was earning a precarious living writing articles on literature. Yeats recognized Synge's genius at once, and often used to quote the words the latter said to him on that occasion. "We should unite stoicism, asceticism and ecstasy: two of them have often come together, but the three, never." Yeats then advised the young writer to leave Paris and return to his native country. "Go to the Aran Islands," he said, "and find a life that has never been expressed." In one of the *Last Poems,* "The Municipal Gallery Revisited," the poet pays a final tribute to both.

Lady Gregory was more of a mother than an Egeria at the first, and even asked Maud Gonne, bluntly, whether she would "marry Willie Yeats." She carried him off to the cottages on her estate to gather folklore under her guidance. Here we must leave Yeats at the outset of the conflict between Helen—Maud Gonne—and Egeria—Lady Gregory. Influenced by Egeria, who polished up his knowledge of rustic speech and familiarized him with the Kiltartan style through her *Cuchulain of Muirthemne,* the poet turned to drama, but the play he wrote—the most significant of all—was inspired by Maud Gonne, who played the part of Cathleen, the *Shan van vocht,* or old woman spirit of Ireland mourning for her four green fields. And swelling the chorus of triumph in the theatre that night in 1902 were the voices of Maud Gonne's "Daughters of Erin," who were to be the pioneers of the revolution in Ireland that would not break out until Easter Monday, fourteen years later, in 1916. A year after the triumph of *Cathleen ni Houlihan* in 1903, Helen married not a poet but a man of action, and the disconsolate Yeats is left to pour out his sorrows in imperishable verse. But he still has Lady Gregory to help him in his struggles in the theatre, and Synge has returned from Aran with a bag of new plays. Yeats is no longer the minstrel who warbles his native woodnotes wild, but a warrior who fights for Synge's *Playboy* upon the Abbey Theatre stage as he would fight for Sean O'Casey's *Plough and the Stars* twenty years later in 1926. If John O'Leary had lived longer and prolonged Yeats's earlier national dream, if Synge's life had not so tragically ended in 1909 as he was writing the end of *Deirdre of the Sorrows,* Yeats's enthusiasm would not have waned as it did when he wrote "September 1913," with its agonized cry:

> Romantic Ireland's dead and gone,
> It's with O'Leary in the grave.

But Yeats himself explained his disillusioned mood in one of his volumes of autobiography, declaring that his only hope lay in the thought "that we who are poets and artists . . . must go from desire to weariness, and so to desire again, and live but for the moment when vision comes to our weariness like terrible lightning in the humility of the brutes."

We present here a selection from the early poems of Yeats, sometimes in their original versions, sometimes as revised by the poet in his early "minstrel" years. Yeats continued to rewrite, especially in middle age, when he attempted to make all his work fit the over-all metaphysical plan he had for his canon. We have chosen to reprint the earlier versions, because of their spontaneous and lyrical quality.

We devotees, who still cherish many vivid memories of the vital simplicity of his old age, when he again remodelled his personality and became a rhapsodist as well as a seer, feel forever tempted to turn to our bookshelves for the first editions of such poems as "The Stolen Child," "The Rose of the World," "Fergus and the Druid," "O'Sullivan Rua to Mary Lavell," and "Cap and Bells," which were written by the sensitive, introspective youth in the eighties and nineties. He was then, as Mathers the magician had warned him, "lost on the path of the chameleon," and pestered by the demons of aestheticism, astrology, magic, and Irish nationalism, yet he still managed to preserve the aloofness and integrity of a cenobite who shuts himself up in his hermitage in the woods.

The Variorum Edition of the Poems of W. B. Yeats,[6] edited by Peter Allt and Russell K. Alspach, is an invaluable possession for the Yeatsian who would see the poet's life mirrored in the changes he wrought in his poems over the years.

In his last five years deeper disillusion fell upon the poet when he saw all that he and Lady Gregory had built up

---

[6] New York: The Macmillan Company, 1957.

during the active civic years after the Anglo-Irish war, and the Irish Civil War of 1922, crumble away and perish on the dust heap as the nations girded themselves for the Second World War. Then it was significant to observe how his mind returned at moments to the early minstrel phase, and some of our most precious memories recall him in an "unbuttoned" mood, evoking ancient Dublin scenes of Michael Moran and his ragamuffin verses, or else in the palatial drawing-room of the Athenaeum in London, chanting at the top of his voice at his white-bearded friend, Sturge Moore, the minstrel poem "The Wild Old Wicked Man."

Walter Starkie

UNIVERSITY OF CALIFORNIA

THE CELTIC TWILIGHT

Time drops in decay
Like a candle burnt out.
And the mountains and woods
Have their day, have their day;
But, kindly old rout
Of the fire-born moods,
You pass not away.

THE HOSTING OF THE SIDHE

The host is riding from Knocknarea,
And over the grave of Clooth-na-bare;
Caolte tossing his burning hair,
And Niamh calling, "Away, come away;
Empty your heart of its mortal dream.
The winds awaken, the leaves whirl round,
Our cheeks are pale, our hair is unbound,
Our breasts are heaving, our eyes are a-gleam,
Our arms are waving, our lips are apart;
And if any gaze on our rushing band,
We come between him and the deed of his hand,
We come between him and the hope of his heart."
The host is rushing 'twixt night and day;
And where is there hope or deed as fair?
Caolte tossing his burning hair,
And Niamh calling, "Away, come away."

THIS BOOK

I

I HAVE desired, like every artist, to create a little world out of the beautiful, pleasant, and significant things of this marred and clumsy world, and to show in a vision something of the face of Ireland to any of my own people who would look where I bid them. I have therefore written down accurately and candidly much that I have heard and seen, and, except by way of commentary, nothing that I have merely imagined. I have, however, been at no pains to separate my own beliefs from those of the peasantry, but have rather let my men and women, dhouls and faeries, go their way unoffended or defended by any argument of mine. The things a man has heard and seen are threads of life, and if he pull them carefully from the confused distaff of memory, any who will can weave them into whatever garments of belief please them best. I too have woven my garment like another, but I shall try to keep warm in it, and shall be well content if it do not unbecome me.

Hope and Memory have one daughter and her name is Art, and she has built her dwelling far from the desperate field where men hang out their garments upon forked boughs to be banners of battle. O beloved daughter of Hope and Memory, be with me for a little.   1893.

II

I have added a few more chapters in the manner of the old ones, and would have added others, but one loses, as one grows older, something of the lightness of one's dreams; one begins to take life up in both hands, and to care more for the fruit than the flower, and that is no great loss perhaps. In these new chapters, as in the old ones, I have invented nothing but my comments and one or two deceitful sentences that may keep some poor story-teller's commerce with the devil and his angels, or the like, from being known among his neighbours. I shall publish in a little while a big book about the commonwealth of faery, and shall try to make it systematical and learned enough to buy pardon for this handful of dreams.   1902.

W. B. YEATS.

A TELLER OF TALES

MANY of the tales in this book were told me by one Paddy Flynn, a little bright-eyed old man, who lived in a leaky and one-roomed cabin in the village of Ballisodare, which is, he was wont to say, "the most gentle"—whereby he meant faery—"place in the whole of County Sligo." Others hold it, however, but second to Drumcliff and Drumahair. The first time I saw him he was cooking mushrooms for himself; the next time he was asleep under a hedge, smiling in his sleep. He was indeed always cheerful, though I thought I could see in his eyes (swift as the eyes of a rabbit, when they peered out of their wrinkled holes) a melancholy which was well-nigh a portion of their joy; the visionary melancholy of purely instinctive natures and of all animals.

And yet there was much in his life to depress him, for

in the triple solitude of age, eccentricity, and deafness, he went about much pestered by children. It was for this very reason perhaps that he ever recommended mirth and hopefulness. He was fond, for instance, of telling how Collumcille cheered up his mother. "How are you to-day, mother?" said the saint. "Worse," replied the mother. "May you be worse to-morrow," said the saint. The next day Collumcille came again, and exactly the same conversation took place, but the third day the mother said, "Better, thank God." And the saint replied, "May you be better to-morrow." He was fond too of telling how the Judge smiles at the last day alike when he rewards the good and condemns the lost to unceasing flames. He had many strange sights to keep him cheerful or to make him sad. I asked him had he ever seen the faeries, and got the reply, "Am I not annoyed with them?" I asked too if he had ever seen the banshee. "I have seen it," he said, "down there by the water, batting the river with its hands."

I have copied this account of Paddy Flynn, with a few verbal alterations, from a note-book which I almost filled with his tales and sayings, shortly after seeing him. I look now at the note-book regretfully, for the blank pages at the end will never be filled up. Paddy Flynn is dead; a friend of mine gave him a large bottle of whiskey, and though a sober man at most times, the sight of so much liquor filled him with a great enthusiasm, and he lived upon it for some days and then died. His body, worn out with old age and hard times, could not bear the drink as in his young days. He was a great teller of tales, and unlike our common romancers, knew how to empty heaven, hell, and purgatory, faeryland and earth, to people his stories. He did not live in a shrunken world, but knew of no less ample circumstance than did Homer himself. Perhaps the Gaelic people shall by his like bring back again the ancient simplicity and amplitude of imagination. What is literature but the expression of moods by the vehicle of symbol and incident? And are there not moods which need heaven, hell, purgatory, and faeryland for their expression, no less than this dilapidated earth? Nay, are there not moods which shall find no expression unless there be men who dare to mix heaven, hell, purgatory, and faeryland together, or even to set the heads of beasts to the bodies of men, or to thrust the souls of men into the heart of rocks? Let us go forth, the tellers of tales, and seize whatever prey the heart long for, and have no fear. Everything exists, everything is true, and the earth is only a little dust under our feet.

BELIEF AND UNBELIEF

THERE are some doubters even in the western villages. One woman told me last Christmas that she did not believe either in hell or in ghosts. Hell she thought was merely an invention got up by the priest to keep people good; and ghosts would not be permitted, she held, to go "trapsin about the earth" at their own free will; "but there are faeries," she added, "and little leprechauns, and water-horses, and fallen angels." I have met also a man with a mohawk Indian tattooed upon his arm, who held exactly similar beliefs and unbeliefs. No matter what one doubts one never doubts the faeries, for, as the man with the mohawk Indian on his arm said to me, "they stand to reason." Even the official mind does not escape this faith.

A little girl who was at service in the village of Grange, close under the seaward slopes of Ben Bulben, suddenly disappeared one night about three years ago. There was at once great excitement in the neighbourhood, because it was rumoured that the faeries had taken her. A villager was said to have long struggled to hold her from them, but at last they prevailed, and he found nothing in his hands but a broomstick. The local constable was applied to, and he at once instituted a house-to-house search, and at the same time advised the people to burn all the *bucalauns* (ragweed) on the field she vanished from, because *bucalauns* are sacred to the faeries. They spent the whole night burning them, the constable repeating spells the while. In the morning the little girl was found, the story goes, wan-

dering in the field. She said the faeries had taken her away
a great distance, riding on a faery horse. At last she saw a
big river, and the man who had tried to keep her from
being carried off was drifting down it—such are the topsy-
turvydoms of faery glamour—in a cockleshell. On the way
her companions had mentioned the names of several people who were about to die shortly in the village.

Perhaps the constable was right. It is better doubtless
to believe much unreason and a little truth than to deny
for denial's sake truth and unreason alike, for when we do
this we have not even a rush candle to guide our steps,
not even a poor sowlth to dance before us on the marsh,
and must needs fumble our way into the great emptiness
where dwell the mis-shapen dhouls. And after all, can
we come to so great evil if we keep a little fire on our
hearths and in our souls, and welcome with open hand
whatever of excellent come to warm itself, whether it be
man or phantom, and do not say too fiercely, even to the
dhouls themselves, "Be ye gone"? When all is said and
done, how do we not know but that our own unreason may
be better than another's truth? for it has been warmed on
our hearths and in our souls, and is ready for the wild bees
of truth to hive in it, and make their sweet honey. Come
into the world again, wild bees, wild bees!

MORTAL HELP

ONE hears in the old poems of men taken away to help
the gods in a battle, and Cuchullan won the goddess Fand
for a while, by helping her married sister and her sister's
husband to overthrow another nation of the Land of Prom-
ise. I have been told, too, that the people of faery cannot
even play at hurley unless they have on either side some
mortal, whose body, or whatever has been put in its place,
as the story-teller would say, is asleep at home. Without

mortal help they are shadowy and cannot even strike the balls. One day I was walking over some marshy land in Galway with a friend when we found an old, hard-featured man digging a ditch. My friend had heard that this man had seen a wonderful sight of some kind, and at last we got the story out of him. When he was a boy he was working one day with about thirty men and women and boys. They were beyond Tuam and not far from Knock-na-gur. Presently they saw, all thirty of them, and at a distance of about half-a-mile, some hundred and fifty of the people of faery. There were two of them, he said, in dark clothes like people of our own time, who stood about a hundred yards from one another, but the others wore clothes of all colours, "bracket" or chequered, and some with red waistcoats.

He could not see what they were doing, but all might have been playing hurley, for "they looked as if it was that." Sometimes they would vanish, and then he would almost swear they came back out of the bodies of the two men in dark clothes. These two men were of the size of living men, but the others were small. He saw them for about half-an-hour, and then the old man he and those about him were working for took up a whip and said, "Get on, get on, or we will have no work done!" I asked if he saw the faeries too, "Oh, yes, but he did not want work he was paying wages for to be neglected." He made everybody work so hard that nobody saw what happened to the faeries.   1902.

A VISIONARY

A YOUNG man came to see me at my lodgings the other night, and began to talk of the making of the earth and the heavens and much else. I questioned him about his life and his doings. He had written many poems and painted many mystical designs since we met last, but latterly had neither written nor painted, for his whole heart was set upon making his mind strong, vigorous, and calm, and the emotional life of the artist was bad for him, he feared. He recited his poems readily, however. He had them all in his memory. Some indeed had never been written down. They, with their wild music as of winds blowing in the reeds,[1] seemed to me the very inmost voice of Celtic sadness, and of Celtic longing for infinite things the world has never seen. Suddenly it seemed to me that he was peering about him a little eagerly. "Do you see anything, X——?" I said. "A shining, winged woman, covered by her long hair, is standing near the doorway," he answered, or some such words. "Is it the influence of some living person who thinks of us, and whose thoughts appear to us in that symbolic form?" I said; for I am well instructed in the ways of the visionaries and in the fashion of their speech. "No," he replied; "for if it were the thoughts of a person who is alive I should feel the living influence in my living body, and my heart would beat and my breath would fail. It is a spirit. It is some one who is dead or who has never lived."

I asked what he was doing, and found he was clerk in a large shop. His pleasure, however, was to wander about upon the hills, talking to half-mad and visionary peasants, or to persuade queer and conscience-stricken persons to deliver up the keeping of their troubles into his care. Another night, when I was with him in his own lodging, more than one turned up to talk over their beliefs and disbeliefs, and sun them as it were in the subtle light of his mind. Sometimes visions come to him as he talks with them, and he is rumoured to have told divers people true matters of their past days and distant friends, and left them hushed with dread of their strange teacher, who seems scarce more than a boy, and is so much more subtle than the oldest among them.

The poetry he recited me was full of his nature and his visions. Sometimes it told of other lives he believes himself

---

[1] I wrote this sentence long ago. This sadness now seems to me a part of all peoples who preserve the moods of the ancient peoples of the world. I am not so pre-occupied with the mystery of Race as I used to be, but leave this sentence and other sentences like it unchanged. We once believed them, and have, it may be, not grown wiser.

to have lived in other centuries, sometimes of people he had talked to, revealing them to their own minds. I told him I would write an article upon him and it, and was told in turn that I might do so if I did not mention his name, for he wished to be always "unknown, obscure, impersonal." Next day a bundle of his poems arrived, and with them a note in these words: "Here are copies of verses you said you liked. I do not think I could ever write or paint any more. I prepare myself for a cycle of other activities in some other life. I will make rigid my roots and branches. It is not now my turn to burst into leaves and flowers."

The poems were all endeavours to capture some high, impalpable mood in a net of obscure images. There were fine passages in all, but these were often embedded in thoughts which have evidently a special value to his mind, but are to other men the counters of an unknown coinage. To them they seem merely so much brass or copper or tarnished silver at the best. At other times the beauty of the thought was obscured by careless writing as though he had suddenly doubted if writing was not a foolish labour. He had frequently illustrated his verses with drawings, in which an imperfect anatomy did not altogether hide extreme beauty of feeling. The faeries in whom he believes have given him many subjects, notably Thomas of Ercildoune sitting motionless in the twilight while a young and beautiful creature leans softly out of the shadow and whispers in his ear. He had delighted above all in strong effects of colour: spirits who have upon their heads instead of hair the feathers of peacocks; a phantom reaching from a swirl of flame towards a star; a spirit passing with a globe of iridescent crystal—symbol of the soul—half shut within his hand. But always under this largess of colour lay some tender homily addressed to man's fragile hopes. This spiritual eagerness draws to him all those who, like himself, seek for illumination or else mourn for a joy that has gone. One of these especially comes to mind. A winter or two ago he spent much of the night walking up and down upon the mountain talking to an old peasant who, dumb to most men, poured out his cares for him. Both were unhappy: X—— because he had then first decided that art and poetry were not for him, and the old peasant because his life was ebbing out with no achievement remaining and no hope

left him. Both how Celtic! how full of striving after a something never to be completely expressed in word or deed.
The peasant was wandering in his mind with prolonged
sorrow. Once he burst out with "God possesses the heavens
—God possesses the heavens—but He covets the world";
and once he lamented that his old neighbours were gone,
and that all had forgotten him: they used to draw a chair
to the fire for him in every cabin, and now they said, "Who
is that old fellow there?" "The fret [Irish for doom] is
over me," he repeated, and then went on to talk once more
of God and heaven. More than once also he said, waving
his arm towards the mountain, "Only myself knows what
happened under the thorn-tree forty years ago"; and as he
said it the tears upon his face glistened in the moonlight.

This old man always rises before me when I think of
X——. Both seek—one in wandering sentences, the other
in symbolic pictures and subtle allegoric poetry—to express
a something that lies beyond the range of expression; and
both, if X—— will forgive me, have within them the vast
and vague extravagance that lies at the bottom of the Celtic
heart. The peasant visionaries that are, the landlord duel-
ists that were, and the whole hurly-burly of legends—Cuchulain fighting the sea for two days until the waves pass
over him and he dies, Caolte storming the palace of the
gods, Oisin seeking in vain for three hundred years to ap-
pease his insatiable heart with all the pleasures of faeryland, these two mystics walking up and down upon the
mountains uttering the central dreams of their souls in no
less dream-laden sentences, and this mind that finds them
so interesting—all are a portion of that great Celtic phan-
tasmagoria whose meaning no man has discovered, nor any
angel revealed.

VILLAGE GHOSTS

IN the great cities we see so little of the world, we drift into our minority. In the little towns and villages there are no minorities; people are not numerous enough. You must see the world there, perforce. Every man is himself a class; every hour carries its new challenge. When you pass the inn at the end of the village you leave your favourite whimsy behind you; for you will meet no one who can share it. We listen to eloquent speaking, read books and write them, settle all the affairs of the universe. The dumb village multitudes pass on unchanging; the feel of the spade in the hand is no different for all our talk: good seasons and bad follow each other as of old. The dumb multitudes are no more concerned with us than is the old horse peering through the rusty gate of the village pound. The ancient map-makers wrote across unexplored regions, "Here are lions." Across the villages of fishermen and turners of the earth, so different are these from us, we can write but one line that is certain, "Here are ghosts."

My ghosts inhabit the village of H——, in Leinster. History has in no manner been burdened by this ancient village, with its crooked lanes, its old abbey churchyard full of long grass, its green background of small fir-trees, and its quay, where lie a few tarry fishing-luggers. In the annals of entomology it is well known. For a small bay lies westward a little, where he who watches night after night may see a certain rare moth fluttering along the edge of the tide, just at the end of evening or the beginning of dawn. A hundred years ago it was carried here from Italy by smugglers in a cargo of silks and laces. If the moth-hunter would throw down his net, and go hunting for ghost tales or tales of the faeries and such-like children of Lillith, he would have need for far less patience.

To approach the village at night a timid man requires great strategy. A man was once heard complaining, "By the cross of Jesus! how shall I go? If I pass by the hill of Dunboy old Captain Burney may look out on me. If I go round by the water, and up by the steps, there is the headless one and another on the quays, and a new one under

he old churchyard wall. If I go right round the other way,
Mrs. Stewart is appearing at Hillside Gate, and the devil
himself is in the Hospital Lane."

I never heard which spirit he braved, but feel sure it was
not the one in the Hospital Lane. In cholera times a shed
had been there set up to receive patients. When the need
had gone by, it was pulled down, but ever since the ground
where it stood has broken out in ghosts and demons and
faeries. There is a farmer at H——, Paddy B—— by
name—a man of great strength, and a teetotaller. His wife
and sister-in-law, musing on his great strength, often wonder what he would do if he drank. One night when passing
through the Hospital Lane, he saw what he supposed at
first to be a tame rabbit; after a little he found that it was
a white cat. When he came near, the creature slowly began
to swell larger and larger, and as it grew he felt his own
strength ebbing away, as though it were sucked out of him.
He turned and ran.

By the Hospital Lane goes the "Faeries Path." Every
evening they travel from the hill to the sea, from the sea
to the hill. At the sea end of their path stands a cottage.
One night Mrs. Arbunathy, who lived there, left her door
open, as she was expecting her son. Her husband was
asleep by the fire; a tall man came in and sat beside him.
After he had been sitting there for a while, the woman
said, "In the name of God, who are you?" He got up and
went out, saying, "Never leave the door open at this hour,
or evil may come to you." She woke her husband and told
him. "One of the good people has been with us," said he.

Probably the man braved Mrs. Stewart at Hillside Gate.
When she lived she was the wife of the Protestant clergy-
man. "Her ghost was never known to harm any one," say
the village people; "it is only doing a penance upon the
earth." Not far from Hillside Gate, where she haunted, appeared for a short time a much more remarkable spirit. Its
haunt was the bogeen, a green lane leading from the western end of the village. I quote its history at length: a typical
village tragedy. In a cottage at the village end of the bogeen
lived a house-painter, Jim Montgomery, and his wife. They
had several children. He was a little dandy, and came of
a higher class than his neighbours. His wife was a very big
woman. Her husband, who had been expelled from the

village choir for drink, gave her a beating one day. Her sister heard of it, and came and took down one of the window shutters—Montgomery was neat about everything, and had shutters on the outside of every window—and beat him with it, being big and strong like her sister. He threatened to prosecute her; she answered that she would break every bone in his body if he did. She never spoke to her sister again, because she had allowed herself to be beaten by so small a man. Jim Montgomery grew worse and worse: his wife soon began to have not enough to eat. She told no one, for she was very proud. Often, too, she would have no fire on a cold night. If any neighbours came in she would say she had let the fire out because she was just going to bed. The people about often heard her husband beating her, but she never told any one. She got very thin. At last one Saturday there was no food in the house for herself and the children. She could bear it no longer, and went to the priest and asked him for some money. He gave her thirty shillings. Her husband met her, and took the money, and beat her. On the following Monday she got very ill, and sent for a Mrs. Kelly. Mrs. Kelly, as soon as she saw her, said, "My woman, you are dying," and sent for the priest and the doctor. She died in an hour. After her death, as Montgomery neglected the children, the landlord had them taken to the workhouse. A few nights after they had gone, Mrs. Kelly was going home through the bogeen when the ghost of Mrs. Montgomery appeared and followed her. It did not leave her until she reached her own house. She told the priest, Father S——, a noted antiquarian, and could not get him to believe her. A few nights afterwards Mrs. Kelly again met the spirit in the same place. She was in too great terror to go the whole way, but stopped at a neighbour's cottage midway, and asked them to let her in. They answered they were going to bed. She cried out, "In the name of God let me in, or I will break open the door." They opened, and so she escaped from the ghost. Next day she told the priest again. This time he believed, and said it would follow her until she spoke to it.

She met the spirit a third time in the bogeen. She asked what kept it from its rest. The spirit said that its children must be taken from the workhouse, for none of its relations were ever there before, and that three masses were to be said for the repose of its soul. "If my husband does not believe you," she said, "show him that," and touched Mrs. Kelly's wrist with three fingers. The places where they touched swelled up and blackened. She then vanished. For a time Montgomery would not believe that his wife had appeared: "she would not show herself to Mrs. Kelly," he said—"she with respectable people to appear to." He was convinced by the three marks, and the children were taken from the workhouse. The priest said the masses, and the shade must have been at rest, for it has not since appeared. Some time afterwards Jim Montgomery died in the workhouse, having come to great poverty through drink.

I know some who believe they have seen the headless ghost upon the quay, and one who, when he passes the old cemetery wall at night, sees a woman with white borders to her cap[1] creep out and follow him. The apparition only leaves him at his own door. The villagers imagine that she follows him to avenge some wrong. "I will haunt you when I die" is a favourite threat. His wife was once half-scared to death by what she considers a demon in the shape of a dog.

These are a few of the open-air spirits; the more domestic of their tribe gather within-doors, plentiful as swallows under southern eaves.

One night a Mrs. Nolan was watching by her dying child in Fluddy's Lane. Suddenly there was a sound of knocking heard at the door. She did not open, fearing it was some unhuman thing that knocked. The knocking ceased. After a little the front-door and then the back-door were burst open, and closed again. Her husband went to see what was wrong. He found both doors bolted. The child died. The doors were again opened and closed as before. Then Mrs. Nolan remembered that she had forgotten to leave window or door open, as the custom is, for the departure of the soul. These strange openings and closings and knockings were warnings and reminders from the spirits who attend the dying.

[1] I wonder why she had white borders to her cap. The old Mayo woman, who has told me so many tales, has told me that her brother-in-law saw "a woman with white borders to her cap going around the stacks in a field, and soon after he got a hurt, and he died in six months."

The house ghost is usually a harmless and well-meaning creature. It is put up with as long as possible. It brings good luck to those who live with it. I remember two children who slept with their mother and sisters and brothers in one small room. In the room was also a ghost. They sold herrings in the Dublin streets, and did not mind the ghost much, because they knew they would always sell their fish easily while they slept in the "ha'nted" room.

I have some acquaintance among the ghost-seers of western villages. The Connaught tales are very different from those of Leinster. These H—— spirits have a gloomy, matter-of-fact way with them. They come to announce a death, to fulfil some obligation, to revenge a wrong, to pay their bills even—as did a fisherman's daughter the other day—and then hasten to their rest. All things they do decently and in order. It is demons, and not ghosts, that transform themselves into white cats or black dogs. The people who tell the tales are poor, serious-minded fishing people, who find in the doings of the ghosts the fascination of fear. In the western tales is a whimsical grace, a curious extravagance. The people who recount them live in the most wild and beautiful scenery, under a sky ever loaded and fantastic with flying clouds. They are farmers and labourers, who do a little fishing now and then. They do not fear the spirits too much to feel an artistic and humorous pleasure in their doings. The ghosts themselves share in their quaint hilarity. In one western town, on whose deserted wharf the grass grows, these spirits have so much vigour that, when a misbeliever ventured to sleep in a haunted house, I have been told they flung him through the window, and his bed after him. In the surrounding villages the creatures use the most strange disguises. A dead old gentleman robs the cabbages of his own garden in the shape of a large rabbit. A wicked sea-captain stayed for years inside the plaster of a cottage wall, in the shape of a snipe, making the most horrible noises. He was only dislodged when the wall was broken down; then out of the solid plaster the snipe rushed away whistling.

"DUST HATH CLOSED HELEN'S EYE"

I

I HAVE been lately to a little group of houses, not many enough to be called a village, in the barony of Kiltartan in County Galway, whose name, Ballylee, is known through all the west of Ireland. There is the old square castle, Ballylee, inhabited by a farmer and his wife, and a cottage where their daughter and their son-in-law live, and a little mill with an old miller, and old ash-trees throwing green shadows upon a little river and great stepping-stones. I went there two or three times last year to talk to the miller about Biddy Early, a wise woman that lived in Clare some years ago, and about her saying, "There is a cure for all evil between the two mill-wheels of Ballylee," and to find out from him or another whether she meant the moss between the running waters or some other herb. I have been there this summer, and I shall be there again before it is autumn, because Mary Hynes, a beautiful woman whose name is still a wonder by turf fires, died there sixty years ago; for our feet would linger where beauty has lived its life of sorrow to make us understand that it is not of the world. An old man brought me a little way from the mill and the castle, and down a long, narrow boreen that was nearly lost in brambles and sloe bushes, and he said, "That is the little old foundation of the house, but the most of it is taken for building walls, and the goats have ate those bushes that are growing over it till they've got cranky, and they won't grow any more. They say she was the handsomest girl in Ireland, her skin was like dribbled snow"——he meant driven snow, perhaps,——"and she had blushes in her cheeks. She had five handsome brothers, but all are gone now!" I talked to him about a poem in Irish, Raftery, a famous poet, made about her, and how it said, "there is a strong cellar in Ballylee." He said the strong cellar was the great hole where the river sank underground, and he brought me to a deep pool, where an otter hurried away under a grey boulder, and told me that many fish came up out of the dark water at early morning "to taste the fresh water coming down from the hills."

I first heard of the poem from an old woman who lives about two miles further up the river, and who remembers Raftery and Mary Hynes. She says, "I never saw anybody so handsome as she was, and I never will till I die," and that he was nearly blind, and had "no way of living but to go round and to mark some house to go to, and then all the neighbours would gather to hear. If you treated him well he'd praise you, but if you did not, he'd fault you in Irish. He was the greatest poet in Ireland, and he'd make a song about that bush if he chanced to stand under it. There was a bush he stood under from the rain, and he made verses praising it, and then when the water came through he made verses dispraising it." She sang the poem to a friend and to myself in Irish, and every word was audible and expressive, as the words in a song were always, as I think, before music grew too proud to be the garment of words, flowing and changing with the flowing and changing of their energies. The poem is not as natural as the best Irish poetry of the last century, for the thoughts are arranged in a too obviously traditional form, so the old poor half-blind man who made it has to speak as if he were a rich farmer offering the best of everything to the woman he loves, but it has naïve and tender phrases. The friend that was with me has made some of the translation, but some of it has been made by the country people themselves. I think it has more of the simplicity of the Irish verses than one finds in most translations.

Going to Mass by the will of God,
The day came wet and the wind rose;
I met Mary Hynes at the cross of Kiltartan,
And I fell in love with her then and there.

I spoke to her kind and mannerly,
As by report was her own way;
And she said, "Raftery, my mind is easy,
You may come to-day to Ballylee."

When I heard her offer I did not linger,
When her talk went to my heart my heart rose.

We had only to go across the three fields,
We had daylight with us to Ballylee.

The table was laid with glasses and a quart measure,
She had fair hair, and she sitting beside me;
And she said, "Drink, Raftery, and a hundred welcomes,
There is a strong cellar in Ballylee."

O star of light and O sun in harvest,
O amber hair, O my share of the world,
Will you come with me upon Sunday
Till we agree together before all the people?

I would not grudge you a song every Sunday evening,
Punch on the table, or wine if you would drink it,
But, O King of Glory, dry the roads before me,
Till I find the way to Ballylee.

There is sweet air on the side of the hill
When you are looking down upon Ballylee;
When you are walking in the valley picking nuts and
        blackberries,
There is music of the birds in it and music of the Sidhe.

What is the worth of greatness till you have the light
Of the flower of the branch that is by your side?
There is no god to deny it or to try and hide it,
She is the sun in the heavens who wounded my heart.

There was no part of Ireland I did not travel,
From the rivers to the tops of the mountains,
To the edge of Lough Greine whose mouth is hidden,
And I saw no beauty but was behind hers.

Her hair was shining, and her brows were shining too;
Her face was like herself, her mouth pleasant and sweet.
She is the pride, and I give her the branch,
She is the shining flower of Ballylee.

It is Mary Hynes, the calm and easy woman,
Has beauty in her mind and in her face.
If a hundred clerks were gathered together,
They could not write down a half of her ways.

An old weaver, whose son is supposed to go away among the Sidhe (the faeries) at night, says, "Mary Hynes was the most beautiful thing ever made. My mother used to tell me about her, for she'd be at every hurling, and wherever she was she was dressed in white. As many as eleven men asked her in marriage in one day, but she wouldn't have any of them. There was a lot of men up beyond Kilbecanty one night, sitting together drinking, and talking of her, and one of them got up and set out to go to Ballylee and see her; but Cloon Bog was open then, and when he came to it he fell into the water, and they found him dead there in the morning. She died of the fever that was before the famine." Another old man says he was only a child when he saw her, but he remembered that "the strongest man that was among us, one John Madden, got his death of the head of her, cold he got crossing rivers in the night-time to get to Ballylee." This is perhaps the man the other remembered, for tradition gives the one thing many shapes. There is an old woman who remembers her, at Derrybrien among the Echtge hills, a vast desolate place, which has changed little since the old poem said, "the stag upon the cold summit of Echtge hears the cry of the wolves," but still mindful of many poems and of the dignity of ancient speech. She says, "The sun and the moon never shone on anybody so handsome, and her skin was so white that it looked blue, and she had two little blushes on her cheeks." And an old wrinkled woman who lives close by Ballylee, and has told me many tales of the Sidhe, says, "I often saw Mary Hynes, she was handsome indeed. She had two bunches of curls beside her cheeks, and they were the colour of silver. I saw Mary Molloy that was drowned in the river beyond, and Mary Guthrie that was in Ardrahan, but she took the sway of them both, a very comely creature. I was at her wake too—she had seen too much of the world. She was a kind creature. One day I was coming home through that field beyond, and I was tired, and who should come out but the Poisin Glegeal (the shining flower), and she gave me a glass of new milk." This old woman meant no more than some beautiful bright colour by the colour of silver, for though I knew an old man —he is dead now—who thought she might know "the cure for all the evils in the world," that the Sidhe knew, she has seen too little gold to know its colour. But a man by the shore at Kinvara, who is too young to remember Mary Hynes, says, "Everybody says there is no one at all to be seen now so handsome; it is said she had beautiful hair, the colour of gold. She was poor, but her clothes every day were the same as Sunday, she had such neatness. And if she went to any kind of a meeting, they would all be killing one another for a sight of her, and there was a great many in love with her, but she died young. It is said that no one that has a song made about them will ever live long."

Those who are much admired are, it is held, taken by the Sidhe, who can use ungoverned feeling for their own ends, so that a father, as an old herb doctor told me once, may give his child into their hands, or a husband his wife. The admired and desired are only safe if one says "God bless them" when one's eyes are upon them. The old woman that sang the song thinks, too, that Mary Hynes was "taken," as the phrase is, "for they have taken many that are not handsome, and why would they not take her? And people came from all parts to look at her, and maybe there were some that did not say 'God bless her.' " An old man who lives by the sea at Duras has as little doubt that she was taken, "for there are some living yet can remember her coming to the pattern[1] there beyond, and she was said to be the handsomest girl in Ireland." She died young because the gods loved her, for the Sidhe are the gods, and it may be that the old saying, which we forget to understand literally, meant her manner of death in old times. These poor countrymen and countrywomen in their beliefs, and in their emotions, are many years nearer to that old Greek world, that set beauty beside the fountain of things, than are our men of learning. She "had seen too much of the world"; but these old men and women, when they tell of her, blame another and not her, and though they can be hard, they grow gentle as the old men of Troy grew gentle when Helen passed by on the walls.

The poet who helped her to so much fame has himself a great fame throughout the west of Ireland. Some think that Raftery was half blind, and say, "I saw Raftery, a dark man, but he had sight enough to see her," or the like,

---

[1] A "pattern," or "patron," is a festival in honour of a saint.

but some think he was wholly blind, as he may have been at the end of his life. Fable makes all things perfect in their kind, and her blind people must never look on the world and the sun. I asked a man I met one day, when I was looking for a pool *na mna Sidhe* where women of faery have been seen, how Raftery could have admired Mary Hynes so much if he had been altogether blind? He said, "I think Raftery was altogether blind, but those that are blind have a way of seeing things, and have the power to know more, and to feel more, and to do more, and to guess more than those that have their sight, and a certain wit and a certain wisdom is given to them." Everybody, indeed, will tell you that he was very wise, for was he not only blind but a poet? The weaver whose words about Mary Hynes I have already given, says, "His poetry was the gift of the Almighty, for there are three things that are the gift of the Almighty—poetry and dancing and principles. That is why in the old times an ignorant man coming down from the hillside would be better behaved and have better learning than a man with education you'd meet now, for they got it from God"; and a man at Coole says, "When he put his finger to one part of his head, everything would come to him as if it was written in a book"; and an old pensioner at Kiltartan says, "He was standing under a bush one time, and he talked to it, and it answered him back in Irish. Some say it was the bush that spoke, but it must have been an enchanted voice in it, and it gave him the knowledge of all the things of the world. The bush withered up afterwards, and it is to be seen on the roadside now between this and Rahasine." There is a poem of his about a bush, which I have never seen, and it may have come out of the cauldron of fable in this shape.

A friend of mine met a man once who had been with him when he died, but the people say that he died alone, and one Maurteen Gillane told Dr. Hyde that all night long a light was seen streaming up to heaven from the roof of the house where he lay, and "that was the angels who were with him"; and all night long there was a great light in the hovel, "and that was the angels who were waking him. They gave that honour to him because he was so good a poet, and sang such religious songs." It may be that in a few years Fable, who changes mortalities to immortalities in her cauldron, will have changed Mary Hynes and Raftery to perfect symbols of the sorrow of beauty and of the magnificence and penury of dreams. 1900.

II

When I was in a northern town awhile ago, I had a long talk with a man who had lived in a neighbouring country district when he was a boy. He told me that when a very beautiful girl was born in a family that had not been noted for good looks, her beauty was thought to have come from the Sidhe, and to bring misfortune with it. He went over the names of several beautiful girls that he had known, and said that beauty had never brought happiness to anybody. It was a thing, he said, to be proud of and afraid of. I wish I had written out his words at the time, for they were more picturesque than my memory of them. 1902.

A KNIGHT OF THE SHEEP

AWAY to the north of Ben Bulben and Cope's mountain lives "a strong farmer," a knight of the sheep they would have called him in the Gaelic days. Proud of his descent from one of the most fighting clans of the Middle Ages, he is a man of force alike in his words and in his deeds. There is but one man that swears like him, and this man lives far away upon the mountain. "Father in Heaven, what have I done to deserve this?" he says when he has lost his pipe; and no man but he who lives on the mountain can rival his language on a fair day over a bargain. He is passionate and abrupt in his movements, and when angry tosses his white beard about with his left hand.

One day I was dining with him when the servant-maid announced a certain Mr. O'Donnell. A sudden silence fell upon the old man and upon his two daughters. At last the eldest daughter said somewhat severely to her father, "Go and ask him to come in and dine." The old man went out, and then came in looking greatly relieved, and said, "He says he will not dine with us." "Go out," said the daughter, "and ask him into the back parlour, and give him some whiskey." Her father, who had just finished his dinner, obeyed sullenly, and I heard the door of the back parlour—a little room where the daughters sat and sewed during the evening—shut to behind the men. The daughter then turned to me and said, "Mr. O'Donnell is the tax-gatherer, and last year he raised our taxes, and my father was very angry, and when he came, brought him into the dairy, and sent the dairy-woman away on a message, and then swore at him a great deal. 'I will teach you, sir,' O'Donnell replied, 'that the law can protect its officers'; but my father reminded him that he had no witness. At last my father got tired, and sorry too, and said he would show him a short way home. When they were half-way to the main road they came on a man of my father's who was ploughing, and this somehow brought back remembrance of the wrong. He sent the man away on a message, and began to swear at the tax-gatherer again. When I heard of it I was disgusted that he should have made such a fuss over a miserable creature like O'Donnell; and when I heard a few weeks ago that O'Donnell's only son had died and left him heart-broken, I resolved to make my father be kind to him next time he came."

She then went out to see a neighbour, and I sauntered towards the back parlour. When I came to the door I heard angry voices inside. The two men were evidently getting on to the tax again, for I could hear them bandying figures to and fro. I opened the door; at sight of my face the farmer was reminded of his peaceful intentions, and asked me if I knew where the whiskey was. I had seen him put it into the cupboard, and was able therefore to find it and get it out, looking at the thin, grief-struck face of the tax-gatherer. He was rather older than my friend, and very much more feeble and worn, and of a very different type. He was not like him, a robust, successful man, but rather one of those whose feet find no resting-place upon the earth. I recognized one of the children of reverie, and said, "You are doubtless of the stock of the old O'Donnells. I know well the hole in the river where their treasure lies buried under the guard of a serpent with many heads." "Yes, sur," he replied, "I am the last of a line of princes."

We then fell to talking of many commonplace things, and my friend did not once toss up his beard, but was very friendly. At last the gaunt old tax-gatherer got up to go, and my friend said, "I hope we will have a glass together next year." "No, no," was the answer, "I shall be dead next year." "I too have lost sons," said the other in quite a gentle voice. "But your sons were not like my son." And then the two men parted, with an angry flush and bitter hearts, and had I not cast between them some common words or other, might not have parted, but have fallen rather into an angry discussion of the value of their dead sons. If I had not pity for all the children of reverie I should have let them fight it out, and would now have many a wonderful oath to record.

The knight of the sheep would have had the victory, for no soul that wears this garment of blood and clay can surpass him. He was but once beaten; and this is his tale of how it was. He and some farm hands were playing at cards in a small cabin that stood against the end of a big barn. A wicked woman had once lived in this cabin. Suddenly one of the players threw down an ace and began to swear without any cause. His swearing was so dreadful that the others stood up, and my friend said, "All is not right here; there is a spirit in him." They ran to the door that led into the barn to get away as quickly as possible. The wooden bolt would not move, so the knight of the sheep took a saw which stood against the wall near at hand, and sawed through the bolt, and at once the door flew open with a bang, as though some one had been holding it, and they fled through.

AN ENDURING HEART

ONE day a friend of mine was making a sketch of my Knight of the Sheep. The old man's daughter was sitting by, and, when the conversation drifted to love and love-making, she said, "Oh, father, tell him about your love affair." The old man took his pipe out of his mouth, and said, "Nobody ever marries the woman he loves," and then, with a chuckle, "There were fifteen of them I liked better than the woman I married," and he repeated many women's names. He went on to tell how when he was a lad he had worked for his grandfather, his mother's father, and was called (my friend has forgotten why) by his grand-father's name, which we will say was Doran. He had a great friend, whom I shall call John Byrne; and one day he and his friend went to Queenstown to await an emigrant ship, that was to take John Byrne to America. When they were walking along the quay, they saw a girl sitting on a seat, crying miserably, and two men standing up in front of her quarrelling with one another. Doran said, "I think I know what is wrong. *That* man will be her brother, and *that* man will be her lover, and the brother is sending her to America to get her away from the lover. How she is crying! but I think I could console her myself." Presently the lover and brother went away, and Doran began to walk up and down before her, saying, "Mild weather, Miss," or the like. She answered him in a little while, and the three began to talk together. The emigrant ship did not arrive for some days; and the three drove about on outside cars very innocently and happily, seeing everything that was to be seen. When at last the ship came, and Doran had to break it to her that he was not going to America, she cried more after him than after the first lover. Doran whispered to Byrne as he went aboard ship, "Now, Byrne, I don't grudge her to you, but don't marry young."

When the story got to this, the farmer's daughter joined in mockingly with, "I suppose you said that for Byrne's good, father." But the old man insisted that he *had* said it for Byrne's good; and went on to tell how, when he got a letter telling of Byrne's engagement to the girl, he wrote him the same advice. Years passed by, and he heard nothing; and though he was now married, he could not keep from wondering what she was doing. At last he went to America to find out, and though he asked many people for tidings, he could get none. More years went by, and his wife was dead, and he well on in years, and a rich farmer with not a few great matters on his hands. He found an excuse in some vague business to go out to America again, and to begin his search again. One day he fell into talk with an Irishman in a railway carriage, and asked him, as his way was, about emigrants from this place and that, and at last, "Did you ever hear of the miller's daughter from Innis Rath?" and he named the woman he was looking for. "Oh yes," said the other, "she is married to a friend of mine, John MacEwing. She lives at such-and-such a street in Chicago." Doran went to Chicago and knocked at her door. She opened the door herself, and was "not a bit changed." He gave her his real name, which he had taken again after his grandfather's death, and the name of the man he had met in the train. She did not recognize him, but asked him to stay to dinner, saying that her husband would be glad to meet anybody who knew that old friend of his. They talked of many things, but for all their talk, I do not know why, and perhaps he did not know why, he never told her who he was. At dinner he asked her about Byrne, and she put her head down on the table and began to cry, and she cried so he was afraid her husband might be angry. He was afraid to ask what had happened to Byrne, and left soon after, never to see her again.

When the old man had finished the story, he said, "Tell that to Mr. Yeats, he will make a poem about it, perhaps." But the daughter said, "Oh no, father. Nobody could make a poem about a woman like that." Alas! I have never made the poem, perhaps because my own heart, which has loved Helen and all the lovely and fickle women of the world, would be too sore. There are things it is well not to ponder over too much, things that bare words are the best suited for. 1902.

THE SORCERERS

IN Ireland we hear but little of the darker powers,[1] and come across any who have seen them even more rarely, for the imagination of the people dwells rather upon the fantastic and capricious, and fantasy and caprice would lose the freedom which is their breath of life, were they to unite them either with evil or with good. And yet the wise are of opinion that wherever man is, the dark powers who would feed his rapacities are there too, no less than the bright beings who store their honey in the cells of his heart, and the twilight beings who flit hither and thither, and that they encompass him with a passionate and melancholy multitude. They hold, too, that he who by long desire or through accident of birth possesses the power of piercing into their hidden abode can see them there, those who were once men or women full of a terrible vehemence, and those who have never lived upon the earth, moving slowly and with a subtler malice. The dark powers cling about us, it is said, day and night, like bats upon an old tree; and that we do not hear more of them is merely because the darker kinds of magic have been but little practised. I have indeed come across very few persons in Ireland who try to communicate with evil powers, and the few I have met keep their purpose and practice wholly hidden from those among whom they live. They are mainly small clerks and the like, and meet for the purpose of their art in a room hung with black hangings. They would not admit me into this room, but finding me not altogether ignorant of the arcane science, showed gladly elsewhere what they would do. "Come to us," said their leader, a clerk in a large flour-mill, "and we will show you spirits who will talk to you face to face, and in shapes as solid and heavy as our own."

I had been talking of the power of communicating in states of trance with the angelical and faery beings,—the children of the day and of the twilight—and he had been

---

[1] I know better now. We have the dark powers much more than I thought, but not as much as the Scottish, and yet I think the imagination of the people does dwell chiefly upon the fantastic and capricious.

contending that we should only believe in what we can see and feel when in our ordinary everyday state of mind. "Yes," I said, "I will come to you," or some such words; "but I will not permit myself to become entranced, and will therefore know whether these shapes you talk of are any the more to be touched and felt by the ordinary senses than are those I talk of." I was not denying the power of other beings to take upon themselves a clothing of mortal substance, but only that simple invocations, such as he spoke of, seemed unlikely to do more than cast the mind into trance, and thereby bring it into the presence of the powers of day, twilight, and darkness.

"But," he said, "we have seen them move the furniture hither and thither, and they go at our bidding, and help or harm people who know nothing of them." I am not giving the exact words, but as accurately as I can the substance of our talk.

On the night arranged I turned up about eight, and found the leader sitting alone in almost total darkness in a small back room. He was dressed in a black gown, like an inquisitor's dress in an old drawing, that left nothing of him visible except his eyes, which peered out through two small round holes. Upon the table in front of him was a brass dish of burning herbs, a large bowl, a skull covered with painted symbols, two crossed daggers, and certain implements shaped like quern stones, which were used to control the elemental powers in some fashion I did not discover. I also put on a black gown, and remember that it did not fit perfectly, and that it interfered with my movements considerably. The sorcerer then took a black cock out of a basket, and cut its throat with one of the daggers, letting the blood fall into the large bowl. He opened a book and began an invocation, which was certainly not English, and had a deep guttural sound. Before he had finished, another of the sorcerers, a man of about twenty-five, came in, and having put on a black gown also, seated himself at my left hand. I had the invoker directly in front of me, and soon began to find his eyes, which glittered through the small holes in his hood, affecting me in a curious way. I struggled hard against their influence, and my head began to ache. The invocation continued, and nothing happened for the first few minutes. Then the invoker got up and extinguished the light in the hall, so that no glimmer might come through the slit under the door. There was now no light except from the herbs on the brass dish, and no sound except from the deep guttural murmur of the invocation.

Presently the man at my left swayed himself about, and cried out, "O god! O god!" I asked him what ailed him, but he did not know he had spoken. A moment after he said he could see a great serpent moving about the room, and became considerably excited. I saw nothing with any definite shape, but thought that black clouds were forming about me. I felt I must fall into a trance if I did not struggle against it, and that the influence which was causing this trance was out of harmony with itself, in other words, evil. After a struggle I got rid of the black clouds, and was able to observe with my ordinary senses again. The two sorcerers now began to see black and white columns moving about the room, and finally a man in a monk's habit, and they became greatly puzzled because I did not see these things also, for to them they were as solid as the table before them. The invoker appeared to be gradually increasing in power, and I began to feel as if a tide of darkness was pouring from him and concentrating itself about me; and now too I noticed that the man on my left hand had passed into a death-like trance. With a last great effort I drove off the black clouds; but feeling them to be the only shapes I should see without passing into a trance, and having no great love for them, I asked for lights, and after the needful exorcism returned to the ordinary world.

I said to the more powerful of the two sorcerers—"What would happen if one of your spirits had overpowered me?" "You would go out of this room," he answered, "with his character added to your own." I asked about the origin of his sorcery, but got little of importance, except that he had learned it from his father. He would not tell me more, for he had, it appeared, taken a vow of secrecy.

For some days I could not get over the feeling of having a number of deformed and grotesque figures lingering about me. The Bright Powers are always beautiful and desirable, and the Dim Powers are now beautiful, now quaintly grotesque, but the Dark Powers express their unbalanced natures in shapes of ugliness and horror.

THE DEVIL

MY old Mayo woman told me one day that something very bad had come down the road and gone into the house opposite, and though she would not say what it was, I knew quite well. Another day she told me of two friends of hers who had been made love to by one whom they believed to be the devil. One of them was standing by the road-side when he came by on horseback, and asked her to mount up behind him, and go riding. When she would not he vanished. The other was out on the road late at night waiting for her young man, when something came flapping and rolling along the road up to her feet. It had the likeness of a newspaper, and presently it flapped up into her face, and she knew by the size of it that it was the *Irish Times*. All of a sudden it changed into a young man, who asked her to go walking with him. She would not, and he vanished.

I know of an old man too, on the slopes of Ben Bulben, who found the devil ringing a bell under his bed, and he went off and stole the chapel bell and rang him out. It may be that this, like the others, was not the devil at all, but some poor wood spirit whose cloven feet had got him into trouble.

HAPPY AND UNHAPPY THEOLOGIANS

I

A MAYO woman once said to me, "I knew a servant girl who hung herself for the love of God. She was lonely for the priest and her society,[1] and hung herself to the

---

[1] The religious society she had belonged to.

banisters with a scarf. She was no sooner dead than she became white as a lily, and if it had been murder or suicide she would have become black as black. They gave her Christian burial, and the priest said she was no sooner dead than she was with the Lord. So nothing matters that you do for the love of God." I do not wonder at the pleasure she has in telling this story, for she herself loves all holy things with an ardour that brings them quickly to her lips. She told me once that she never hears anything described in a sermon that she does not afterwards see with her eyes. She has described to me the gates of Purgatory as they showed themselves to her eyes, but I remember nothing of the description except that she could not see the souls in trouble but only the gates. Her mind continually dwells on what is pleasant and beautiful. One day she asked me what month and what flower were the most beautiful. When I answered that I did not know, she said, "the month of May, because of the Virgin, and the lily of the valley, be-cause it never sinned, but came pure out of the rocks," and then she asked, "what is the cause of the three cold months of winter?" I did not know even that, and so she said, "the sin of man and the vengeance of God." Christ Himself was not only blessed, but perfect in all manly pro-portions in her eyes, so much do beauty and holiness go together in her thoughts. He alone of all men was exactly six feet high, all others are a little more or a little less.

Her thoughts and her sights of the people of faery are pleasant and beautiful too, and I have never heard her call them the Fallen Angels. They are people like ourselves, only better-looking, and many and many a time she has gone to the window to watch them drive their waggons through the sky, waggon behind waggon in long line, or to the door to hear them singing and dancing in the Forth. They sing chiefly, it seems, a song called "The Distant Waterfall," and though they once knocked her down she never thinks badly of them. She saw them most easily when she was in service in King's County, and one morn-ing a little while ago she said to me, "Last night I was wait-ing up for the master and it was a quarter-past eleven. I heard a bang right down on the table. 'King's County all over,' says I, and I laughed till I was near dead. It was a warning I was staying too long. They wanted the place to themselves." I told her once of somebody who saw a faery and fainted, and she said, "It could not have been a faery, but some bad thing, nobody could faint at a faery. It was a demon. I was not afraid when they near put me, and the bed under me, out through the roof. I wasn't afraid either when you were at some work and I heard a thing coming flop-flop up the stairs like an eel, and squealing. It went to all the doors. It could not get in where I was. I would have sent it through the universe like a flash of fire. There was a man in my place, a tearing fellow, and he put one of them down. He went out to meet it on the road, but he must have been told the words. But the faeries are the best neighbours. If you do good to them they will do good to you, but they don't like you to be on their path." Another time she said to me, "They are always good to the poor."

II

There is, however, a man in a Galway village who can see nothing but wickedness. Some think him very holy, and others think him a little crazed, but some of his talk reminds one of those old Irish visions of the Three Worlds, which are supposed to have given Dante the plan of the *Divine Comedy*. But I could not imagine this man seeing Paradise. He is especially angry with the people of faery, and describes the faun-like feet that are so common among them, who are indeed children of Pan, to prove them children of Satan. He will not grant that "they carry away women, though there are many that say so," but he is certain that they are "as thick as the sands of the sea about us, and they tempt poor mortals."

He says, "There is a priest I know of was looking along the ground like as if he was hunting for something, and a voice said to him, 'If you want to see them you'll see enough of them,' and his eyes were opened and he saw the ground thick with them. Singing they do be sometimes, and dancing, but all the time they have cloven feet." Yet he was so scornful of unchristian things for all their dancing and singing that he thinks that "you have only to bid them begone and they will go. It was one night," he says, "after walking back from Kinvara and down by the wood beyond I felt one coming beside me, and I could feel the horse he was riding on and the way he lifted his legs, but they do not make a sound like the hoofs of a horse. So I stopped and turned around and said, very loud, 'Be off!' and he went and never troubled me after. And I knew a man who was dying, and one came on his bed, and he cried out to it, 'Get out of that, you unnatural animal!' and it left him. Fallen angels they are, and after the fall God said, 'Let there be Hell,' and there it was in a moment." An old woman who was sitting by the fire joined in as he said this with "God save us, it's a pity He said the word, and there might have been no Hell the day," but the seer did not notice her words. He went on, "And then he asked the devil what would he take for the souls of all the people. And the devil said nothing would satisfy him but the blood of a virgin's son, so he got that, and then the gates of Hell were opened." He understood the story, it seems, as if it were some riddling old folk tale.

"I have seen Hell myself. I had a sight of it one time in a vision. It had a very high wall around it, all of metal, and an archway, and a straight walk into it, just like what 'ud be leading into a gentleman's orchard, but the edges were not trimmed with box, but with red-hot metal. And inside the wall there were cross-walks, and I'm not sure what there was to the right, but to the left there were five great furnaces, and they full of souls kept there with great chains. So I turned short and went away, and in turning I looked again at the wall, and I could see no end to it.

"And another time I saw Purgatory. It seemed to be in a level place, and no walls around it, but it all one bright blaze, and the souls standing in it. And they suffer near as much as in Hell, only there are no devils with them there, and they have the hope of Heaven.

"And I heard a call to me from there, 'Help me to come out o' this!' And when I looked it was a man I used to know in the army, an Irishman, and from this county, and I believe him to be a descendant of King O'Connor of Athenry.

"So I stretched out my hand first, but then I called out, 'I'd be burned in the flames before I could get within three yards of you.' So then he said, 'Well, help me with your prayers,' and so I do.

"And Father Connellan says the same thing, to help the dead with your prayers, and he's a very clever man to make a sermon, and has a great deal of cures made with the Holy Water he brought back from Lourdes." 1902.

THE LAST GLEEMAN

MICHAEL MORAN was born about 1794 off Black Pitts, in the Liberties of Dublin, in Faddle Alley. A fortnight after birth he went stone blind from illness, and became thereby a blessing to his parents, who were soon able to send him to rhyme and beg at street corners and at the bridges over the Liffey. They may well have wished that their quiver were full of such as he, for, free from the interruption of sight, his mind became a perfect echoing chamber, where every movement of the day and every change of public passion whispered itself into rhyme or quaint saying. By the time he had grown to manhood he was the admitted rector of all the ballad-mongers of the Liberties. Madden, the weaver, Kearney, the blind fiddler from Wicklow, Martin from Meath, M'Bride from heaven knows where, and that M'Grane, who in after days, when the true Moran was no more, strutted in borrowed plumes, or rather in borrowed rags, and gave out that there had never been any Moran but himself, and many another, did homage before him, and held him chief of all their tribe. Nor despite his blindness did he find any difficulty in getting a wife, but rather was able to pick and choose, for he was just that mixture of ragamuffin and of genius which is dear to the heart of woman, who, perhaps because she is wholly conventional herself, loves the unexpected, the crooked, the bewildering. Nor did he lack, despite his rags, many excellent things, for it is remembered that he ever loved caper sauce, going so far indeed in his honest indignation at its absence upon one occasion as to fling a leg

of mutton at his wife. He was not, however, much to look
at, with his coarse frieze coat with its cape and scalloped
edge, his old corduroy trousers and great brogues, and his
stout stick made fast to his wrist by a thong of leather: and
he would have been a woeful shock to the gleeman Mac-
Conglinne, could that friend of kings have beheld him in
prophetic vision from the pillar stone at Cork. And yet
though the short cloak and the leather wallet were no more,
he was a true gleeman, being alike poet, jester, and news-
man of the people. In the morning when he had finished
his breakfast, his wife or some neighbour would read the
newspaper to him, and read on and on until he interrupted
with, "That'll do—I have me meditations"; and from these
meditations would come the day's store of jest and rhyme.
He had the whole Middle Ages under his frieze coat.

He had not, however, MacConglinne's hatred of the
Church and clergy, for when the fruit of his meditations
did not ripen well, or when the crowd called for something
more solid, he would recite or sing a metrical tale or ballad
of saint or martyr or of Biblical adventure. He would stand
at a street corner, and when a crowd had gathered would
begin in some such fashion as follows (I copy the record
of one who knew him)—"Gather round me, boys, gather
round me. Boys, am I standin' in puddle? am I standin' in
wet?" Thereon several boys would cry, "Ah, no! yez not!
yer in a nice dry place. Go on with *St. Mary;* go on with
Moses"—each calling for his favourite tale. Then Moran,
with a suspicious wriggle of his body and a clutch at
his rags, would burst out with "All me buzzim friends are
turned backbiters"; and after a final "If yez don't drop
your coddin' and diversion I'll lave some of yez a case," by
way of warning to the boys, begin his recitation, or perhaps
still delay, to ask, "Is there a crowd round me now?
Any blackguard heretic around me?" The best-known
of his religious tales was *St. Mary of Egypt,* a long poem
of exceeding solemnity, condensed from the much longer
work of a certain Bishop Coyle. It told how a fast woman
of Egypt, Mary by name, followed pilgrims to Jerusalem
for no good purpose, and then, turning penitent on finding
herself withheld from entering the Temple by supernatural
interference, fled to the desert and spent the remainder of
her life in solitary penance. When at last she was at the

point of death, God sent Bishop Zozimus to hear her confession, give her the last sacrament, and with the help
of a lion, whom He sent also, dig her grave. The poem
has the intolerable cadence of the eighteenth century, but
was so popular and so often called for that Moran was soon
nicknamed Zozimus, and by that name is he remembered.
He had also a poem of his own called *Moses,* which went
a little nearer poetry without going very near. But he could
ill brook solemnity, and before long parodied his own
verses in the following ragamuffin fashion:

> In Egypt's land, contagious to the Nile,
> King Pharaoh's daughter went to bathe in style.
> She tuk her dip, then walked unto the land,
> To dry her royal pelt she ran along the strand.
> A bulrush tripped her, whereupon she saw
> A smiling babby in a wad o' straw.
> She tuk it up, and said with accents mild,
> " 'Tare-and-agers, girls, which av yez owns the child?"

His humorous rhymes were, however, more often quips
and cranks at the expense of his contemporaries. It was
his delight, for instance, to remind a certain shoemaker,
noted alike for display of wealth and for personal un-
cleanness, of his inconsiderable origin in a song of which
but the first stanza has come down to us:

> At the dirty end of Dirty Lane,
> Liv'd a dirty cobbler, Dick Maclane;
> His wife was in the old king's reign
>   A stout brave orange-woman.
> On Essex Bridge she strained her throat,
> And six-a-penny was her note.
> But Dickey wore a bran-new coat,
>   He got among the yeomen.
> He was a bigot, like his clan,
> And in the streets he wildly sang,
> O Roly, toly, toly raid, with his old jade.

He had troubles of divers kinds, and numerous interlopers
to face and put down. Once an officious peeler arrested
him as a vagabond, but was triumphantly routed amid the

laughter of the court, when Moran reminded his worship of the precedent set by Homer, who was also, he declared, a poet, and a blind man, and a beggarman. He had to face a more serious difficulty as his fame grew. Various imitators started up upon all sides. A certain actor, for instance, made as many guineas as Moran did shillings by mimicking his sayings and his songs and his getup upon the stage. One night this actor was at supper with some friends, when dispute arose as to whether his mimicry was overdone or not. It was agreed to settle it by an appeal to the mob. A forty-shilling supper at a famous coffeehouse was to be the wager. The actor took up his station at Essex Bridge, a great haunt of Moran's, and soon gathered a small crowd. He had scarce got through "In Egypt's land, contagious to the Nile," when Moran himself came up, followed by another crowd. The crowds met in great excitement and laughter. "Good Christians," cried the pretender, "is it possible that any man would mock the poor dark man like that?"

"Who's that? It's some imposhterer," replied Moran.

"Begone, you wretch! it's you'ze the imposhterer. Don't you fear the light of heaven being struck from your eyes for mocking the poor dark man?"

"Saints and angels, is there no protection against this? You're a most inhuman-blaguard to try to deprive me of my honest bread this way," replied poor Moran.

"And you, you wretch, won't let me go on with the beautiful poem. Christian people, in your charity won't you beat this man away? he's taking advantage of my darkness."

The pretender, seeing that he was having the best of it, thanked the people for their sympathy and protection, and went on with the poem, Moran listening for a time in bewildered silence. After a while Moran protested again with:

"Is it possible that none of yez can know me? Don't yez see it's myself; and that's some one else?"

"Before I can proceed any further in this lovely story," interrupted the pretender, "I call on yez to contribute your charitable donations to help me to go on."

"Have you no sowl to be saved, you mocker of heaven?" cried Moran, put completely beside himself by this last injury. "Would you rob the poor as well as desave the world? O, was ever such wickedness known?"

"I leave it to yourselves, my friends," said the pretender, "to give to the real dark man, that you all know so well, and save me from that schemer," and with that he collected some pennies and half-pence. While he was doing so, Moran started his *Mary of Egypt,* but the indignant crowd seizing his stick were about to belabour him, when they fell back bewildered anew by his close resemblance to himself. The pretender now called to them to "just give him a grip of that villain, and he'd soon let him know who the imposhterer was!" They led him over to Moran, but instead of closing with him he thrust a few shillings into his hand, and turning to the crowd explained to them he was indeed but an actor, and that he had just gained a wager, and so departed amid much enthusiasm, to eat the supper he had won.

In April 1846 word was sent to the priest that Michael Moran was dying. He found him at 15 (now 14½) Patrick Street, on a straw bed, in a room full of ragged ballad-singers come to cheer his last moments. After his death the ballad-singers, with many fiddles and the like, came again and gave him a fine wake, each adding to the merriment whatever he knew in the way of rann, tale, old saw, or quaint rhyme. He had had his day, had said his prayers and made his confession, and why should they not give him a hearty send-off? The funeral took place the next day. A good party of his admirers and friends got into the hearse with the coffin, for the day was wet and nasty. They had not gone far when one of them burst out with "It's cruel cowld, isn't it?" "Garra'," replied another, "we'll all be as stiff as the corpse when we get to the berrin-ground." "Bad cess to him," said a third; "I wish he'd held out another month until the weather got dacent." A man called Carroll thereupon produced a half-pint of whiskey, and they all drank to the soul of the departed. Unhappily, however, the hearse was over-weighted, and they had not reached the cemetery before the spring broke, and the bottle with it.

Moran must have felt strange and out of place in that other kingdom he was entering, perhaps while his friends were drinking in his honour. Let us hope that some kindly middle region was found for him, where he can call dishevelled angels about him with some new and more rhythmical form of his old

> Gather round me, boys, will yez
>   Gather round me?
> And hear what I have to say
>   Before ould Salley brings me
> My bread and jug of tay;

and fling outrageous quips and cranks at cherubim and seraphim. Perhaps he may have found and gathered, ragamuffin though he be, the Lily of High Truth, the Rose of Far-sought Beauty, for whose lack so many of the writers of Ireland, whether famous or forgotten, have been futile as the blown froth upon the shore.

REGINA, REGINA PIGMEORUM, VENI

ONE night a middle-aged man, who had lived all his life far from the noise of cab-wheels, a young girl, a relation of his, who was reported to be enough of a seer to catch a glimpse of unaccountable lights moving over the fields among the cattle, and myself, were walking along a far western sandy shore. We talked of the Forgetful People as the faery people are sometimes called, and came in the midst of our talk to a notable haunt of theirs, a shallow cave amidst black rocks, with its reflection under it in the wet sea sand. I asked the young girl if she could see anything, for I had quite a number of things to ask the Forgetful People. She stood still for a few minutes, and I saw that she was passing into a kind of waking trance, in which the cold sea breeze no longer troubled her, nor the dull boom of the sea distracted her attention. I then called aloud the names of the great faeries, and in a moment or two she said that she could hear music far inside the rocks, and then a sound of confused talking, and of people stamping their feet as if to applaud some unseen performer. Up to this my other friend had been walking to and fro some yards off, but now he passed close to us, and as he did so said suddenly that we were going to be interrupted, for he heard the laughter of children somewhere beyond the rocks. We were, however, quite alone. The spirits of the place had begun to cast their influence over him also. In a moment he was corroborated by the girl, who said that bursts of laughter had begun to mingle with the music, the confused talking, and the noise of feet. She next saw a bright light streaming out of the cave, which seemed to have grown much deeper, and a quantity of little people,[1] in various coloured dresses, red predominating, dancing to a tune which she did not recognize.

I then bade her call out to the queen of the little people to come and talk with us. There was, however, no answer to her command. I therefore repeated the words aloud myself, and in a moment a very beautiful tall woman came out of the cave. I too had by this time fallen into a kind of trance, in which what we call the unreal had begun to take upon itself a masterful reality, and was able to see the faint gleam of golden ornaments, the shadowy blossom of dim hair. I then bade the girl tell this tall queen to marshal her followers according to their natural divisions, that we might see them. I found as before that I had to repeat the command myself. The creatures then came out of the cave, and drew themselves up, if I remember rightly, in four bands. One of these bands carried quicken boughs in their hands, and another had necklaces made apparently of serpents' scales, but their dress I cannot remember, for I was quite absorbed in that gleaming woman. I asked her to tell the seer whether these caves were the greatest faery haunts in the neighbourhood. Her lips moved, but the answer was inaudible. I bade the seer lay her hand upon the breast of the queen, and after that she heard every word quite distinctly. No, this was not the greatest faery haunt, for there was a greater one a little further ahead. I then asked her whether it was true that she and her people

---

[1] The people and faeries in Ireland are sometimes as big as we are, sometimes bigger, and sometimes, as I have been told, about three feet high. The Old Mayo woman I so often quote, thinks that it is something in our eyes that makes them seem big or little.

carried away mortals, and if so, whether they put another soul in the place of the one they had taken? "We change the bodies," was her answer. "Are any of you ever born into mortal life?" "Yes." "Do I know any who were among your people before birth?" "You do." "Who are they?" "It would not be lawful for you to know." I then asked whether she and her people were not "dramatizations of our moods"? "She does not understand," said my friend, "but says that her people are much like human beings, and do most of the things human beings do." I asked her other questions, as to her nature, and her purpose in the universe, but only seemed to puzzle her. At last she appeared to lose patience, for she wrote this message for me upon the sands —the sands of vision, not the grating sands under our feet—"Be careful, and do not seek to know too much about us." Seeing that I had offended her, I thanked her for what she had shown and told, and let her depart again into her cave. In a little while the young girl awoke out of her trance, and felt again the cold wind of the world, and began to shiver.

I tell these things as accurately as I can, and with no theories to blur the history. Theories are poor things at the best, and the bulk of mine have perished long ago. I love better than any theory the sound of the Gate of Ivory, turning upon its hinges, and hold that he alone who has passed the rose-strewn threshold can catch the far glimmer of the Gate of Horn. It were perhaps well for us all if we would but raise the cry Lilly the astrologer raised in Windsor Forest, "Regina, Regina Pigmeorum, Veni," and remember with him, that God visiteth His children in dreams. Tall, glimmering queen, come near, and let me see again the shadowy blossom of thy dim hair.

"AND FAIR, FIERCE WOMEN"

ONE day a woman that I know came face to face with heroic beauty, that highest beauty which Blake says changes least from youth to age, a beauty which has been fading out of the arts, since that decadence we call progress, set voluptuous beauty in its place. She was standing at the window, looking over to Knocknarea where Queen Maive is thought to be buried, when she saw, as she has told me, "the finest woman you ever saw travelling right across from the mountain and straight to her." The woman had a sword by her side and a dagger lifted up in her hand, and was dressed in white, with bare arms and feet. She looked "very strong, but not wicked," that is, not cruel. The old woman had seen the Irish giant, and "though he was a fine man," he was nothing to this woman, "for he was round, and could not have stepped out so soldierly"; "she was like Mrs. ———" a stately lady of the neighbourhood, "but she had no stomach on her, and was slight and broad in the shoulders, and was handsomer than any one you ever saw; she looked about thirty." The old woman covered her eyes with her hands, and when she uncovered them the apparition had vanished. The neighbours were "wild with her," she told me, because she did not wait to find out if there was a message, for they were sure it was Queen Maive, who often shows herself to the pilots. I asked the old woman if she had seen others like Queen Maive, and she said, "Some of them have their hair down, but they look quite different, like the sleepy-looking ladies one sees in the papers. Those with their hair up are like this one. The others have long white dresses, but those with their hair up have short dresses, so that you can see their legs right up to the calf." After some careful questioning I found that they wore what might very well be a kind of buskin; she went on, "They are fine and dashing looking, like the men one sees riding their horses in twos and threes on the slopes of the mountains with their swords swinging." She repeated over and over, "There is no such race living now, none so finely proportioned," or the like, and then said, "The present Queen [1] is a nice, pleasant-looking woman, but she is not like her. What makes me think so little of the ladies is that I see none as they be," meaning as the spirits. "When I think of her and of the ladies now, they are like little children running about without knowing how to put their clothes on right. Is it the ladies? Why, I would not call them women at all." The other day a friend of mine questioned an old woman in a Galway workhouse about Queen Maive, and was told that "Queen Maive was handsome, and overcame all her enemies with a hazel stick, for the hazel is blessed, and the best weapon that can be got. You might walk the world with it," but she grew "very disagreeable in the end—oh very disagreeable. Best not to be talking about it. Best leave it between the book and the hearer." My friend thought the old woman had got some scandal about Fergus son of Roy and Maive in her head.

And I myself met once with a young man in the Burren Hills who remembered an old poet who made his poems in Irish and had met when he was young, the young man said, one who called herself Maive, and said she was a queen "among them," and asked him if he would have money or pleasure. He said he would have pleasure, and she gave him her love for a time, and then went from him, and ever after he was very mournful. The young man had often heard him sing the poem of lamentation that he made, but could only remember that it was "very mournful," and that he called her "beauty of all beauties."   1902.

[1] Queen Victoria.

ENCHANTED WOODS

I

LAST summer, whenever I had finished my day's work, I used to go wandering in certain roomy woods, and there I would often meet an old countryman, and talk to him about his work and about the woods, and once or twice a friend came with me to whom he would open his heart more readily than to me. He had spent all his life lopping away the witch elm and the hazel and the privet and the hornbeam from the paths, and had thought much about the natural and supernatural creatures of the wood. He has heard the hedgehog—"grainne oge," he calls him—"grunting like a Christian," and is certain that he steals apples by rolling about under an apple tree until there is an apple sticking to every quill. He is certain too that the cats, of whom there are many in the woods, have a language of their own—some kind of old Irish. He says, "Cats were serpents, and they were made into cats at the time of some great change in the world. That is why they are hard to kill, and why it is dangerous to meddle with them. If you annoy a cat it might claw or bite you in a way that would put poison in you, and that would be the serpent's tooth." Sometimes he thinks they change into wild cats, and then a nail grows on the end of their tails; but these wild cats are not the same as the marten cats, who have been always in the woods. The foxes were once tame, as the cats are now, but they ran away and became wild. He talks of all wild creatures except squirrels—whom he hates—with what seems an affectionate interest, though at times his eyes will twinkle with pleasure as he remembers how he made hedgehogs unroll themselves when he was a boy, by putting a wisp of burning straw under them.

I am not certain that he distinguishes between the natural and supernatural very clearly. He told me the other day that foxes and cats like, above all, to be in the "forths" and lisses after nightfall; and he will certainly pass from some story about a fox to a story about a spirit with less change of voice than when he is going to speak about a marten cat—a rare beast now-a-days. Many years ago he used to work in the garden, and once they put him to sleep in a garden-house where there was a loft full of apples, and all night he could hear people rattling plates and knives and forks over his head in the loft. Once, at any rate, he has seen an unearthly sight in the woods. He says, "One time I was out cutting timber over in Inchy, and about eight o'clock one morning when I got there I saw a girl picking nuts, with her hair hanging down over her shoulders, brown hair, and she had a good, clean face, and she was tall and nothing on her head, and her dress no way gaudy but simple, and when she felt me coming she gathered herself up and was gone as if the earth had swallowed her up. And I followed her and looked for her, but I never could see her again from that day to this, never again." He used the word clean as we would use words like fresh or comely.

Others too have seen spirits in the Enchanted Woods. A labourer told us of what a friend of his had seen in a part of the woods that is called Shanwalla, from some old village that was before the wood. He said, "One evening I parted from Lawrence Mangan in the yard, and he went away through the path in Shanwalla, an' bid me good-night. And two hours after, there he was back again in the yard, an' bid me light a candle that was in the stable. An' he told me that when he got into Shanwalla, a little fellow about as high as his knee, but having a head as big as a man's body, came beside him and led him out of the path an' round about, and at last it brought him to the lime-kiln, and then it vanished and left him."

A woman told me of a sight that she and others had seen by a certain deep pool in the river. She said, "I came over the stile from the chapel, and others along with me; and a great blast of wind came and two trees were bent and broken and fell into the river, and the splash of water out of it went up to the skies. And those that were with me saw many figures, but myself I only saw one, sitting there by the bank where the trees fell. Dark clothes he had on, and he was headless."

A man told me that one day, when he was a boy, he and another boy went to catch a horse in a certain field, full of boulders and bushes of hazel and creeping juniper and rock-roses, that is where the lake side is for a little clear of the woods. He said to the boy that was with him, "I bet a button that if I fling a pebble on to that bush it will stay on it," meaning that the bush was so matted the pebble would not be able to go through it. So he took up "a pebble of cow-dung, and as soon as it hit the bush there came out of it the most beautiful music that ever was heard." They ran away, and when they had gone about two hundred yards they looked back and saw a woman dressed in white, walking round and round the bush. "First it had the form of a woman, and then of a man, and it was going round the bush."

II

I often entangle myself in argument more complicated than even those paths of Inchy as to what is the true nature of apparitions, but at other times I say as Socrates said when they told him a learned opinion about a nymph of the Ilissus, "The common opinion is enough for me." I believe when I am in the mood that all nature is full of people whom we cannot see, and that some of these are ugly or grotesque, and some wicked or foolish, but very many beautiful beyond any one we have ever seen, and that these are not far away when we are walking in pleasant and quiet places. Even when I was a boy I could never walk in a wood without feeling that at any moment I might find before me somebody or something I had long looked for without knowing what I looked for. And now I will at times explore every little nook of some poor coppice with almost anxious footsteps, so deep a hold has this imagination upon me. You too meet with a like imagination, doubtless, somewhere, wherever your ruling stars will have it, Saturn driving you to the woods, or the Moon, it may be, to the edges of the sea. I will not of a certainty believe that there is nothing in the sunset, where our forefathers imagined the dead following their shepherd the sun, or nothing but some vague presence as little moving as nothing. If beauty is not a gateway out of the net we were taken in at our birth, it will not long be beauty, and we will find it better to sit at home by the fire and fatten a lazy body or to run hither and thither in some foolish sport than to look at the finest show that light and shadow ever made among green leaves. I say to myself, when I am well out of that thicket of argument, that they are surely there, the divine people, for only we who have neither simplicity nor wisdom have denied them, and the simple of all times and the wise men of ancient times have seen them and even spoken to them. They live out their passionate lives not far off, as I think, and we shall be among them when we die if we but keep our natures simple and passionate. May it not even be that death shall unite us to all romance, and that some day we shall fight dragons among blue hills, or come to that whereof all romance is but

> Foreshadowings mingled with the images
> Of man's misdeeds in greater days than these,

as the old men thought in *The Earthly Paradise* when they were in good spirits.

1902.

MIRACULOUS CREATURES

THERE are marten cats and badgers and foxes in the Enchanted Woods, but there are of a certainty mightier creatures, and the lake hides what neither net nor line can take. These creatures are of the race of the white stag that flits in and out of the tales of Arthur, and of the evil pig that slew Diarmuid where Ben Bulben mixes with the sea wind. They are the wizard creatures of hope and fear, they are of them that fly and of them that follow among the thickets that are about the Gates of Death. A man I know remembers that his father was one night in the wood of Inchy, "where the lads of Gort used to be stealing rods. He was sitting by the wall, and the dog beside him, and he heard something come running from Owbawn Weir, and he could see nothing, but the sound of its feet on the ground was like the sound of the feet of a deer. And when it passed him, the dog got between him and the wall and scratched at it there as if it was afraid, but still he could see nothing but only hear the sound of hoofs. So when it was passed he turned and came away home. Another time," the man says, "my father told me he was in a boat out on the lake with two or three men from Gort, and one of them had an eel-spear, and he thrust it into the water, and it hit something, and the man fainted and they had to carry him out of the boat to land, and when he came to himself he said that what he struck was like a calf, but whatever it was, it was not fish!" A friend of mine is convinced that these terrible creatures, so common in lakes, were set there in old times by subtle enchanters to watch over the gates of wisdom. He thinks that if we sent our spirits down into the water we would make them of one substance with strange moods of ecstasy and power, and go out it may be to the conquest of the world. We would, however, he believes, have first to outface and perhaps overthrow strange images full of a more powerful life than if they were really alive. It may be that we shall look at them without fear when we have endured the last adventure, that is death.

1902.

ARISTOTLE OF THE BOOKS

THE friend who can get the wood-cutter to talk more readily than he will to anybody else went lately to see his old wife. She lives in a cottage not far from the edge of the woods, and is as full of old talk as her husband. This time she began to talk of Goban, the legendary mason, and his wisdom, but said presently, "Aristotle of the Books, too, was very wise, and he had a great deal of experience, but did not the bees get the better of him in the end? He wanted to know how they packed the comb, and he wasted the better part of a fortnight watching them, and he could not see them doing it. Then he made a hive with a glass cover on it and put it over them, and he thought to see. But when he went and put his eyes to the glass, they had it all covered with wax so that it was as black as the pot; and he was as blind as before. He said he was never rightly kilt till then. They had him that time surely!"

1902.

THE SWINE OF THE GODS

A FEW years ago a friend of mine told me of something that happened to him when he was a young man and out drilling with some Connaught Fenians. They were but a car-full, and drove along a hillside until they came to a quiet place. They left the car and went further up the hill with their rifles, and drilled for a while. As they were coming down again they saw a very thin, long-legged pig of the old Irish sort, and the pig began to follow them. One of them cried out as a joke that it was a fairy pig, and they all began to run to keep up the joke. The pig ran too, and presently, how nobody knew, this mock terror became real terror, and they ran as for their lives. When they got to the car they made the horse gallop as fast as possible, but the pig still followed. Then one of them put up his rifle to fire, but when he looked along the barrel he could see nothing. Presently they turned a corner and came to a village. They told the people of the village what had happened, and the people of the village took pitchforks and spades and the like, and went along the road with them to drive the pig away. When they turned the corner they could not find anything.

1902.

A VOICE

ONE day I was walking over a bit of marshy ground close to Inchy Wood when I felt, all of a sudden, and only for a second, an emotion which I said to myself was the root of Christian mysticism. There had swept over me a sense of weakness, of dependence on a great personal Being somewhere far off yet near at hand. No thought of mine had prepared me for this emotion, for I had been pre-occupied with Ængus and Edain, and with Mannanan, son of the sea. That night I awoke lying upon my back and hearing a voice speaking above me and saying, "No human soul is like any other human soul, and therefore the love of God for any human soul is infinite, for no other soul can satisfy the same need in God." A few nights after this I awoke to see the loveliest people I have ever seen. A young man and a young girl dressed in olive-green raiment, cut like old Greek raiment, were standing at my bedside. I looked at the girl and noticed that her dress was gathered about her neck into a kind of chain, or perhaps into some kind of stiff embroidery which represented ivy-leaves. But what filled me with wonder was the miraculous mildness of her face. There are no such faces now. It was beautiful, as few faces are beautiful, but it had neither, one would think, the light that is in desire or in hope or in fear or in speculation. It was peaceful like the faces of animals, or like mountain pools at evening, so peaceful that it was a little sad. I thought for a moment that she might be the beloved of Ængus, but how could that hunted, alluring, happy, immortal wretch have a face like this? Doubtless she was from among the children of the Moon, but who among them I shall never know.

1902.

KIDNAPPERS

A LITTLE north of the town of Sligo, on the southern side of Ben Bulben, some hundreds of feet above the plain, is a small white square in the limestone. No mortal has ever touched it with his hand; no sheep or goat has ever browsed grass beside it. There is no more inaccessible place upon the earth, and few more encircled by awe to the deep considering. It is the door of faery-land. In the middle of night it swings open, and the unearthly troop rushes out. All night the gay rabble sweep to and fro across the land, invisible to all, unless perhaps where, in some more than commonly "gentle" place—Drumcliff or Druma-hair—the nightcapped heads of faery-doctors may be thrust from their doors to see what mischief the "gentry" are doing. To their trained eyes and ears the fields are covered by red-hatted riders, and the air is full of shrill voices—a sound like whistling, as an ancient Scottish seer has recorded, and wholly different from the talk of the angels, who "speak much in the throat, like the Irish," as Lilly, the astrologer, has wisely said. If there be a new-born baby or new-wed bride in the neighbourhood, the night-capped "doctors" will peer with more than common care, for the unearthly troop do not always return empty-handed. Sometimes a new-wed bride or a new-born baby goes with them into their mountains; the door swings to behind, and the new-born or the new-wed moves henceforth in the bloodless land of Faery; happy enough, but doomed to melt out at the last judgment like bright vapour, for the soul cannot live without sorrow. Through this door of white stone, and the other doors of that land where *geabheadh tu an sonas aer pighin* ("you can buy joy for a penny"), have gone kings, queens, and princes, but so greatly has the power of Faery dwindled, that there are none but peasants in these sad chronicles of mine.

Somewhere about the beginning of last century appeared at the western corner of Market Street, Sligo, where the butcher's shop now is, not a palace, as in Keats's *Lamia,* but an apothecary's shop, ruled over by a certain unaccountable Dr. Opendon. Where he came from, none ever knew. There also was in Sligo, in those days, a woman, Ormsby by name, whose husband had fallen mysteriously sick. The doctors could make nothing of him. Nothing seemed wrong with him, yet weaker and weaker he grew. Away went the wife to Dr. Opendon. She was shown into the shop parlour. A black cat was sitting straight up before the fire. She had just time to see that the side-board was covered with fruit, and to say to herself, "Fruit must be wholesome when the doctor has so much," before Dr. Opendon came in. He was dressed all in black, the same as the cat, and his wife walked behind him dressed in black likewise. She gave him a guinea, and got a little bottle in return. Her husband recovered that time. Meanwhile the black doctor cured many people; but one day a rich patient died, and cat, wife, and doctor all vanished the night after. In a year the man Ormsby fell sick once more. Now he was a goodlooking man, and his wife felt sure the "gentry" were coveting him. She went and called on the "faery-doctor" at Cairnsfoot. As soon as he had heard her tale, he went behind the back door and began muttering, muttering, muttering—making spells. Her husband got well this time also. But after a while he sickened again, the fatal third time, and away went she once more to Cairnsfoot, and out went the faery-doctor behind his back door and began muttering, but soon he came in and told her it was no use —her husband would die; and sure enough the man died, and ever after when she spoke of him Mrs. Ormsby shook her head saying she knew well where he was, and it wasn't in heaven or hell or purgatory either. She probably believed that a log of wood was left behind in his place, but so bewitched that it seemed the dead body of her husband.

She is dead now herself, but many still living remember her. She was, I believe, for a time a servant or else a kind of pensioner of some relations of my own.

Sometimes those who are carried off are allowed after many years—seven usually—a final glimpse of their friends. Many years ago a woman vanished suddenly from a Sligo garden where she was walking with her husband. When her son, who was then a baby, had grown up he received word in some way, not handed down, that his mother was glamoured by faeries, and imprisoned for the time in a house in Glasgow and longing to see him. Glasgow in those days of sailing-ships seemed to the peasant mind almost over the edge of the known world, yet he, being a dutiful son, started away. For a long time he walked the streets of Glasgow; at last down in a cellar he saw his mother working. She was happy, she said, and had the best of good eating, and would he not eat? and therewith laid all kinds of food on the table; but he, knowing well that she was trying to cast on him the glamour by giving him faery food, that she might keep him with her, refused and came home to his people in Sligo.

Some five miles southward of Sligo is a gloomy and tree-bordered pond, a great gathering-place of water-fowl, called, because of its form, the Heart Lake. It is haunted by stranger things than heron, snipe, or wild duck. Out of this lake, as from the white square stone in Ben Bulben, issues an unearthly troop. Once men began to drain it; suddenly one of them raised a cry that he saw his house in flames. They turned round, and every man there saw his own cottage burning. They hurried home to find it was but faery glamour. To this hour on the border of the lake is shown a half-dug trench—the signet of their impiety. A little way from this lake I heard a beautiful and mournful history of faery kidnapping. I heard it from a little old woman in a white cap, who sings to herself in Gaelic, and moves from one foot to the other as though she remembered the dancing of her youth.

A young man going at nightfall to the house of his just married bride, met in the way a jolly company, and with them his bride. They were faeries, and had stolen her as a wife for the chief of their band. To him they seemed only a company of merry mortals. His bride, when she saw her old love, bade him welcome, but was most fearful lest he should eat the faery food, and so be glamoured out of the earth into that bloodless dim nation, wherefore she set him down to play cards with three of the cavalcade; and he played on, realizing nothing until he saw the chief of the band carrying his bride away in his arms. Immediately he started up, and knew that they were faeries; for slowly all that jolly company melted into shadow and night. He hurried to the house of his beloved. As he drew near came to him the cry of the keeners. She had died some time before he came. Some noteless Gaelic poet had made this into a forgotten ballad, some odd verses of which my white-capped friend remembered and sang for me.

Sometimes one hears of stolen people acting as good genii to the living, as in this tale, heard also close by the haunted pond, of John Kirwan of Castle Hacket. The Kirwans[1] are a family much rumoured of in peasant stories, and believed to be the descendants of a man and a spirit. They have ever been famous for beauty, and I have read that the mother of the present Lord Cloncurry was of their tribe.

John Kirwan was a great horse-racing man, and once landed in Liverpool with a fine horse, going racing somewhere in middle England. That evening, as he walked by the docks, a slip of a boy came up and asked where he was stabling his horse. In such and such a place, he answered. "Don't put him there," said the slip of a boy; "that stable will be burnt to-night." He took his horse elsewhere, and sure enough the stable was burnt down. Next day the boy came and asked as reward to ride as his jockey in the coming race, and then was gone. The race-time came round. At the last moment the boy ran forward and mounted, saying, "If I strike him with the whip in my left hand I will lose, but if in my right hand bet all you are worth." For, said Paddy Flynn, who told me the tale, "the left arm is good for nothing. I might go on making the sign of the cross with it, and all that, come Christmas, and a Banshee, or such like, would no more mind than if it was that broom." Well, the slip of a boy struck the horse with his right hand, and John Kirwan cleared the field out. When the race was over, "What can I do for you now?" said he. "Nothing but this," said the boy: "my mother has a cottage on your land—they stole me from the cradle. Be good to her, John Kirwan, and wherever your horses go I will watch that no

[1] I have since heard that it was not the Kirwans, but their predecessors at Castle Hacket, the Hackets themselves, I think, who were descended from a man and a spirit, and were notable for beauty. I imagine that the mother of Lord Cloncurry was descended from the Hackets. It may well be that all through these stories the name of Kirwan has taken the place of the older name. Legend mixes everything together in her cauldron.

ill follows them; but you will never see me more." With that he made himself air, and vanished.

Sometimes animals are carried off—apparently drowned animals more than others. In Claremorris, Galway, Paddy Flynn told me, lived a poor widow with one cow and its calf. The cow fell into the river, and was washed away. There was a man thereabouts who went to a red-haired woman—for such are supposed to be wise in these things —and she told him to take the calf down to the edge of the river, and hide himself and watch. He did as she had told him, and as evening came on the calf began to low, and after a while the cow came along the edge of the river and commenced suckling it. Then, as he had been told, he caught the cow's tail. Away they went at a great pace across hedges and ditches, till they came to a royalty (a name for the little circular ditches, commonly called raths or forts, that Ireland is covered with since Pagan times). Therein he saw walking or sitting all the people who had died out of his village in his time. A woman was sitting on the edge with a child on her knees, and she called out to him to mind what the red-haired woman had told him, and he remembered she had said, Bleed the cow. So he stuck his knife into the cow and drew blood. That broke the spell, and he was able to turn her homeward. "Do not forget the spancel," said the woman with the child on her knees; "take the inside one." There were three spancels on a bush; he took one, and the cow was driven safely home to the widow.

There is hardly a valley or mountainside where folk cannot tell you of some one pillaged from amongst them. Two or three miles from the Heart Lake lives an old woman who was stolen away in her youth. After seven years she was brought home again for some reason or other, but she had no toes left. She had danced them off. Many near the white stone door in Ben Bulben have been stolen away.

It is far easier to be sensible in cities than in many country places I could tell you of. When one walks on those grey roads at evening by the scented elder-bushes of the white cottages, watching the faint mountains gathering the clouds upon their heads, one all too readily discovers, beyond the thin cobweb veil of the senses, those creatures, the goblins, hurrying from the white square stone door to the north, or from the Heart Lake in the south.

THE UNTIRING ONES

IT is one of the great troubles of life that we cannot have any unmixed emotions. There is always something in our enemy that we like, and something in our sweetheart that we dislike. It is this entanglement of moods which makes us old, and puckers our brows and deepens the furrows about our eyes. If we could love and hate with as good heart as the faeries do, we might grow to be long-lived like them. But until that day their untiring joys and sorrows must ever be one-half of their fascination. Love with them never grows weary, nor can the circles of the stars tire out their dancing feet. The Donegal peasants remember this when they bend over the spade, or sit full of the heaviness of the fields beside the griddle at nightfall, and they tell stories about it that it may not be forgotten. A short while ago, they say, two faeries, little creatures, one like a young man, one like a young woman, came to a farmer's house, and spent the night sweeping the hearth and setting all tidy. The next night they came again, and while the farmer was away, brought all the furniture up-stairs into one room, and having arranged it round the walls, for the greater grandeur it seems, they began to dance. They danced on and on, and days and days went by, and all the country-side came to look at them, but still their feet never tired. The farmer did not dare to live at home the while; and after three months he made up his mind to stand it no more, and went and told them that the priest was coming. The little creatures when they heard this went back to their own country, and there their joy shall last as long as the points of the rushes are brown, the people say, and that is until God shall burn up the world with a kiss.

But it is not merely faeries who know untiring days, for there have been men and women who, falling under their enchantment, have attained, perhaps by the right of their God-given spirits, an even more than faery abundance of life and feeling. It seems that when mortals have gone amid those poor happy leaves of the Imperishable Rose of Beauty, blown hither and thither by the winds that awakened the stars, the dim kingdom has acknowledged their birthright, perhaps a little sadly, and given them of its best. Such a mortal was born long ago at a village in the south of Ireland. She lay asleep in a cradle, and her mother sat by rocking her, when a woman of the Sidhe (the faeries) came in, and said that the child was chosen to be the bride of the prince of the dim kingdom, but that as it would never do for his wife to grow old and die while he was still in the first ardour of his love, she would be gifted with a faery life. The mother was to take the glowing log out of the fire and bury it in the garden, and her child would live as long as it remained unconsumed. The mother buried the log, and the child grew up, became a beauty, and married the prince of the faeries, who came to her at nightfall. After seven hundred years the prince died, and another prince ruled in his stead and married the beautiful peasant girl in his turn; and after another seven hundred years he died also, and another prince and another husband came in his stead, and so on until she had had seven husbands. At last one day the priest of the parish called upon her, and told her that she was a scandal to the whole neighbourhood with her seven husbands and her long life. She was very sorry, she said, but she was not to blame, and then she told him about the log, and he went straight out and dug until he found it, and then they burned it, and she died, and was buried like a Christian, and everybody was pleased. Such a mortal too was Clooth-na-bare,[1] who went all over the world seeking a lake deep enough to drown her faery life, of which she had grown weary, leaping from hill to lake and lake to hill, and setting up a cairn of stones wherever her feet lighted, until at last she found the deepest water in the world in little Lough Ia, on the top of the Birds' Mountain at Sligo.

The two little creatures may well dance on, and the

---

[1] Doubtless Clooth-na-bare should be Cailleac Bare, which would mean the old Woman Bare. Bare or Bere or Verah or Dera or Dhera was a very famous person, perhaps the mother of the Gods herself. A friend of mine found her, as he thinks, frequenting Lough Leath, or the Grey Lake on a mountain of the Fews. Perhaps Lough Ia is my mishearing, or the story-teller's mispronunciation of Lough Leath, for there are many Lough Leaths.

woman of the log and Clooth-na-bare sleep in peace, for they have known untrammelled hate and unmixed love, and have never wearied themselves with "yes" and "no," or entangled their feet with the sorry net of "maybe" and "perhaps." The great winds came and took them up into themselves.

EARTH, FIRE AND WATER

SOME French writer that I read when I was a boy, said that the desert went into the heart of the Jews in their wanderings and made them what they are. I cannot remember by what argument he proved them to be even yet the indestructible children of earth, but it may well be that the elements have their children. If we knew the Fire Worshippers better we might find that their centuries of pious observance have been rewarded, and that the fire has given them a little of its nature; and I am certain that the water, the water of the seas and of lakes and of mist and rain, has all but made the Irish after its image. Images form themselves in our minds perpetually as if they were reflected in some pool. We gave ourselves up in old times to mythology, and saw the Gods everywhere. We talked to them face to face, and the stories of that communion are so many that I think they outnumber all the like stories of all the rest of Europe. Even to-day our country people speak with the dead and with some who perhaps have never died as we understand death; and even our educated people pass without great difficulty into the condition of quiet that is the condition of vision. We can make our minds so like still water that beings gather about us that they may see, it may be, their own images, and so live for a moment with a clearer, perhaps even with a fiercer life because of our quiet. Did not the wise Porphyry think that all souls come to be born because of water, and that "even the generation of images in the mind is from water"?   1902.

THE OLD TOWN

I FELL, one night some fifteen years ago, into what seemed the power of faery.

I had gone with a young man and his sister—friends and relations of my own—to pick stories out of an old countryman; and we were coming home talking over what he had told us. It was dark, and our imaginations were excited by his stories of apparitions, and this may have brought us, unknown to us, to the threshold, between sleeping and waking, where Sphinxes and Chimæras sit open-eyed and where there are always murmurings and whisperings. I cannot think that what we saw was an imagination of the waking mind. We had come under some trees that made the road very dark, when the girl saw a bright light moving slowly across the road. Her brother and myself saw nothing, and did not see anything until we had walked for about half-an-hour along the edge of the river and down a narrow lane to some fields where there was a ruined church covered with ivy, and the foundations of what was called "the Old Town," which had been burned down, it was said, in Cromwell's day. We had stood for some few minutes, so far as I can recollect, looking over the fields full of stones and brambles and elder-bushes, when I saw a small bright light on the horizon, as it seemed, mounting up slowly towards the sky; then we saw other faint lights for a minute or two, and at last a bright flame like the flame of a torch moving rapidly over the river. We saw it all in such a dream, and it seems all so unreal, that I have never written of it until now, and hardly ever spoken of it, and even when thinking, because of some unreasoning impulse, I have avoided giving it weight in the argument. Perhaps I have felt that my recollections of things seen when the sense of reality was weakened must be untrustworthy. A few months ago, however, I talked it over with my two friends, and compared their somewhat meagre recollections with my own. That sense of unreality was all the more wonderful because the next day I heard sounds as unaccountable as were those lights, and without any emotion of unreality, and I remember them with perfect distinctness and confidence. The girl was sitting reading under a large old-fashioned mirror, and I was reading and writing a couple of yards away, when I heard a sound as if a shower of peas had been thrown against the mirror, and while I was looking at it I heard the sound again, and presently, while I was alone in the room, I heard a sound as if something much bigger than a pea had struck the wainscoting beside my head. And after that for some days came other sights and sounds, not to me but to the girl, her brother, and the servants. Now it was a bright light, now it was letters of fire that vanished before they could be read, now it was a heavy foot moving about in the seemingly empty house. One wonders whether creatures who live, the country people believe, wherever men and women have lived in earlier times, followed us from the ruins of the old town? or did they come from the banks of the river by the trees where the first light had shone for a moment?   1902.

THE MAN AND HIS BOOTS

THERE was a doubter in Donegal, and he would not hear of ghosts or sheogues, and there was a house in Donegal that had been haunted as long as man could remember, and this is the story of how the house got the better of the man. The man came into the house and lighted a fire in the room under the haunted one, and took off his boots and set them on the hearth, and stretched out his feet and warmed himself. For a time he prospered in his unbelief; but a little while after the night had fallen, and everything had got very dark, one of his boots began to move. It got up off the floor and gave a kind of slow jump towards the door, and then the other boot did the same, and after that the first boot jumped again. And thereupon it struck the man that an invisible being had got into his boots, and was now going away in them. When the boots reached the door they went up-stairs slowly, and then the man heard them go tramp, tramp round the haunted room over his head. A few minutes passed, and he could hear them again upon the stairs, and after that in the passage outside, and then one of them came in at the door, and the other gave a jump past it and came in too. They jumped along towards him, and then one got up and hit him, and afterwards the other hit him, and then again the first hit him, and so on, until they drove him out of the room, and finally out of the house. In this way he was kicked out by his own boots, and Donegal was avenged upon its doubter. It is not recorded whether the invisible being was a ghost or one of the Sidhe, but the fantastic nature of the vengeance is like the work of the Sidhe who live in the heart of fantasy.

A COWARD

One day I was at the house of my friend the strong farmer, who lives beyond Ben Bulben and Cope's mountain, and met there a young lad who seemed to be disliked by the two daughters. I asked why they disliked him, and was told he was a coward. This interested me, for some whom robust children of nature take to be cowards are but men and women with a nervous system too finely made for their life and work. I looked at the lad; but no, that pink-and-white face and strong body had nothing of undue sensibility. After a little he told me his story. He had lived a wild and reckless life, until one day, two years before, he was coming home late at night, and suddenly felt himself sinking in, as it were, upon the ghostly world. For a moment he saw the face of a dead brother rise up before him, and then he turned and ran. He did not stop till he came to a cottage nearly a mile down the road. He flung himself against the door with so much of violence that he broke the thick wooden bolt and fell upon the floor. From that day he gave up his wild life, but was a hopeless coward. Nothing could ever bring him to look, either by day or night, upon the spot where he had seen the face, and he often went two miles round to avoid it; nor could, he said, "the prettiest girl in the country" persuade him to see her home after a party if he were alone. He feared everything, for he had looked at the face no man can see unchanged—the imponderable face of a spirit.

THE THREE O'BYRNES AND THE EVIL FAERIES

IN the dim kingdom there is a great abundance of all excellent things. There is more love there than upon the earth; there is more dancing there than upon the earth; and there is more treasure there than upon the earth. In the beginning the earth was perhaps made to fulfil the desire of man, but now it has got old and fallen into decay. What wonder if we try and pilfer the treasures of that other kingdom!

A friend was once at a village near Sleive League. One day he was straying about a rath called "Cashel Nore." A man with a haggard face and unkempt hair, and clothes falling in pieces, came into the rath and began digging. My friend turned to a peasant who was working near and asked who the man was. "That is the third O'Byrne," was the answer. A few days after he learned this story: A great quantity of treasure had been buried in the rath in pagan times, and a number of evil faeries set to guard it; but some day it was to be found and belong to the family of the O'Byrnes. Before that day three O'Byrnes must find it and die. Two had already done so. The first had dug and dug until at last he had got a glimpse of the stone coffin that contained it, but immediately a thing like a huge hairy dog came down the mountain and tore him to pieces. The next morning the treasure had again vanished deep into the earth. The second O'Byrne came and dug and dug until he found the coffer, and lifted the lid and saw the gold shining within. He saw some horrible sight the next moment, and went raving mad and soon died. The treasure again sank out of sight. The third O'Byrne is now digging. He believes that he will die in some terrible way the moment he finds the treasure, but that the spell will be broken, and the O'Byrne family made rich for ever, as they were of old.

A peasant of the neighbourhood once saw the treasure. He found the shin-bone of a hare lying on the grass. He took it up; there was a hole in it; he looked through the hole, and saw the gold heaped up under the ground. He hurried home to bring a spade, but when he got to the rath again he could not find the spot where he had seen it.

DRUMCLIFF AND ROSSES

DRUMCLIFF and Rosses were, are, and ever shall be, please Heaven! places of unearthly resort. I have lived near by them and in them, time after time, and have gathered thus many a crumb of faery lore. Drumcliff is a wide green valley, lying at the foot of Ben Bulben, the mountain in whose side the square white door swings open at nightfall to loose the faery riders on the world. The great St. Columba himself, the builder of many of the old ruins in the valley, climbed the mountains on one notable day to get near heaven with his prayers. Rosses is a little sea-dividing, sandy plain, covered with short grass, like a green table-cloth, and lying in the foam midway between the round cairn-headed Knocknarea and "Ben Bulben, famous for hawks":

> But for Benbulben and Knocknarea
> Many a poor sailor'd be cast away,

as the rhyme goes.

At the northern corner of Rosses is a little promontory of sand and rocks and grass: a mournful, haunted place. No wise peasant would fall asleep under its low cliff, for he who sleeps here may wake "silly," the "good people" having carried off his soul. There is no more ready short-cut to the dim kingdom than this plovery headland, for, covered and smothered now from sight by mounds of sand, a long cave goes thither "full of gold and silver, and the most beautiful parlours and drawing-rooms." Once, before the sand covered it, a dog strayed in, and was heard yelping helplessly deep underground in a fort far inland. These forts or raths, made before modern history had begun, cover all Rosses and all Columkille. The one where the dog yelped has, like most others, an underground bee-hive chamber in the midst. Once when I was poking about there, an unusually intelligent and "reading" peasant who had come with me, and waited outside, knelt down by the opening, and whispered in a timid voice, "Are you all right, sir?" I had been some little while underground, and he feared I had been carried off like the dog.

No wonder he was afraid, for the fort has long been circled by ill-boding rumours. It is on the ridge of a small hill, on whose northern slope lie a few stray cottages. One night a farmer's young son came from one of them and saw the fort all flaming, and ran towards it, but the "glamour" fell on him, and he sprang on to a fence, cross-legged, and commenced beating it with a stick, for he imagined the fence was a horse, and that all night long he went on the most wonderful ride through the country. In the morning he was still beating his fence, and they carried him home, where he remained a simpleton for three years before he came to himself again. A little later a farmer tried to level the fort. His cows and horses died, and all manner of trouble overtook him, and finally he himself was led home, and left useless with "his head on his knees by the fire to the day of his death."

A few hundred yards southwards of the northern angle of Rosses is another angle having also its cave, though this one is not covered with sand. About twenty years ago a brig was wrecked near by, and three or four fishermen were put to watch the deserted hulk through the darkness. At midnight they saw sitting on a stone at the cave's mouth two red-capped fiddlers fiddling with all their might. The men fled. A great crowd of villagers rushed down to the cave to see the fiddlers, but the creatures had gone.

To the wise peasant the green hills and woods round him are full of never-fading mystery. When the aged countrywoman stands at her door in the evening, and, in her own words, "looks at the mountains and thinks of the goodness of God," God is all the nearer, because the pagan powers are not far: because northward in Ben Bulben, famous for hawks, the white square door swings open at sundown, and those wild unchristian riders rush forth upon the fields, while southward the White Lady, who is doubtless Maive herself, wanders under the broad cloud nightcap of Knocknarea. How may she doubt these things, even though the priest shakes his head at her? Did not a herdboy, no long while since, see the White Lady? She passed so close that the skirt of her dress touched him. "He fell down, and was dead three days." But this is merely the small gossip of faerydom—the little stitches that join this world and the other.

One night as I sat eating Mrs. H——'s soda-bread, her husband told me a longish story, much the best of all I heard in Rosses. Many a poor man from Fin M'Cool to our own days has had some such adventure to tell of, for those creatures, the "good people," love to repeat themselves. At any rate the story-tellers do. "In the times when we used to travel by the canal," he said, "I was coming down from Dublin. When we came to Mullingar the canal ended, and I began to walk, and stiff and fatigued I was after the slowness. I had some friends with me, and now and then we walked, now and then we rode in a cart. So on till we saw some girls milking cows, and stopped to joke with them. After a while we asked them for a drink of milk. 'We have nothing to put it in here,' they said, 'but come to the house with us.' We went home with them, and sat round the fire talking. After a while the others went, and left me, loath to stir from the good fire. I asked the girls for something to eat. There was a pot on the fire, and they took the meat out and put it on a plate, and told me to eat only the meat that came off the head. When I had eaten, the girls went out, and I did not see them again. It grew darker and darker, and there I still sat, loath as ever to leave the good fire, and after a while two men came in, carrying between them a corpse. When I saw them coming I hid behind the door. Says one to the other, putting the corpse on the spit, 'Who'll turn the spit?' Says the other, 'Michael H——, come out of that and turn the meat.' I came out all of a tremble, and began turning the spit. 'Michael H——,' says the one who spoke first, 'if you let it burn we'll have to put you on the spit instead'; and on that they went out. I sat there trembling and turning the corpse till towards midnight. The men came again, and the one said it was burnt, and the other said it was done right. But having fallen out over it, they both said they would do me no harm that time; and, sitting by the fire, one of them cried out: 'Michael H——, can you tell me a story?' 'Divil a one,' said I. On which he caught me by the shoulder, and put me out like a shot. It was a wild blowing night. Never in all my born days did I see such a night—the darkest night that ever came out of the heavens. I did not know where I was for the life of me. So when one of the men came after me and touched me on the shoulder, with a 'Michael H——, can you tell a story now?' 'I can,' says I. In he brought me; and putting me by the fire, says: 'Begin.' 'I have no story but the one,' says I, 'that I was sitting here, and you two men brought in a corpse and put it on the spit, and set me turning it.' 'That will do,' says he; 'ye may go in there and lie down on the bed.' And I went, nothing loath; and in the morning where was I but in the middle of a green field!"

"Drumcliff" is a great place for omens. Before a prosperous fishing season a herring-barrel appears in the midst of a storm-cloud; and at a place called Columkille's Strand, a place of marsh and mire, an ancient boat, with St. Columba himself, comes floating in from sea on a moonlight night: a portent of a brave harvesting. They have their dread portents too. Some few seasons ago a fisherman saw, far on the horizon, renowned Hy Brazel, where he who touches shall find no more labour or care, nor cynic laughter, but shall go walking about under shadiest boscage, and enjoy the conversation of Cuchullin and his heroes. A vision of Hy Brazel forebodes national troubles.

Drumcliff and Rosses are chokeful of ghosts. By bog, road, rath, hillside, sea-border they gather in all shapes: headless women, men in armour, shadow hares, fire-tongued hounds, whistling seals, and so on. A whistling seal sank a ship the other day. At Drumcliff there is a very ancient graveyard. *The Annals of the Four Masters* have this verse about a soldier named Denadhach, who died in 871: "A pious soldier of the race of Con lies under hazel crosses at Drumcliff." Not very long ago an old woman, turning to go into the churchyard at night to pray, saw standing before her a man in armour, who asked her where she was going. It was the "pious soldier of the race of Con," says local wisdom, still keeping watch, with his ancient piety, over the graveyard. Again, the custom is still common hereabouts of sprinkling the doorstep with the blood of a chicken on the death of a very young child, thus (as belief is) drawing into the blood the evil spirits from the too weak soul. Blood is a great gatherer of evil spirits. To cut your hand on a stone on going into a fort is said to be very dangerous.

There is no more curious ghost in Drumcliff or Rosses than the snipe-ghost. There is a bush behind a house in a village that I know well: for excellent reasons I do not say whether in Drumcliff or Rosses or on the slope of Ben Bulben, or even on the plain round Knocknarea. There is a history concerning the house and the bush. A man once lived there who found on the quay of Sligo a package containing three hundred pounds in notes. It was dropped by a foreign sea captain. This my man knew, but said nothing. It was money for freight, and the sea captain, not daring to face his owners, committed suicide in mid-ocean. Shortly afterwards my man died. His soul could not rest. At any rate, strange sounds were heard round his house, though that had grown and prospered since the freight money. The wife was often seen by those still alive out in the garden praying at the bush I have spoken of, for the shade of the dead man appeared there at times. The bush remains to this day: once portion of a hedge, it now stands by itself, for no one dare put spade or pruning-knife about it. As to the strange sounds and voices, they did not cease till a few years ago, when, during some repairs, a snipe flew out of the solid plaster and away; the troubled ghost, say the neighbours, of the note-finder was at last dislodged.

My forebears and relations have lived near Rosses and Drumcliff these many years. A few miles northward I am wholly a stranger, and can find nothing. When I ask for stories of the faeries, my answer is some such as was given me by a woman who lives near a white stone fort—one of the few stone ones in Ireland—under the seaward angle of Ben Bulben: "They always mind their own affairs and I always mind mine": for it is dangerous to talk of the creatures. Only friendship for yourself or knowledge of your forebears will loosen these cautious tongues. My friend, "the sweet Harp-String" (I give no more than his Irish name for fear of gaugers), has the science of unpacking the stubbornest heart, but then he supplies the *potheen*-makers with grain from his own fields. Besides, he is descended from a noted Gaelic magician who raised the "dhoul" in Great Eliza's century, and he has a kind of prescriptive right to hear tell of all kind of other-world creatures. They are almost relations of his, if all people say concerning the parentage of magicians be true.

THE THICK SKULL OF THE FORTUNATE

I

ONCE a number of Icelandic peasantry found a very thick skull in the cemetery where the poet Egil was buried. Its great thickness made them feel certain it was the skull of a great man, doubtless of Egil himself. To be doubly sure they put it on a wall and hit it hard blows with a hammer. It got white where the blows fell but did not break, and they were convinced that it was in truth the skull of the poet, and worthy of every honour. In Ireland we have much kinship with the Icelanders, or "Danes" as we call them and all other dwellers in the Scandinavian countries. In some of our mountainous and barren places, and in our seaboard villages, we still test each other in much the same way the Icelanders tested the head of Egil. We may have acquired the custom from those ancient Danish pirates, whose descendants the people of Rosses tell me still remember every field and hillock in Ireland which once belonged to their forebears, and are able to describe Rosses itself as well as any native. There is one seaboard district known as Roughley, where the men are never known to shave or trim their wild red beards, and where there is a fight ever on foot. I have seen them at a boat-race fall foul of each other, and after much loud Gaelic, strike each other with oars. The first boat had gone aground, and by dint of hitting out with the long oars kept the second boat from passing, only to give the victory to the third. One day the Sligo people say a man from Roughley was tried in Sligo for breaking a skull in a row, and made the defence not unknown in Ireland, that some heads are so thin you cannot be responsible for them. Having turned with a look of passionate contempt towards the solicitor who was prosecuting, and cried, "that little fellow's skull if ye were to hit it would go like an egg-shell," he beamed upon the judge, and said in a wheedling voice, "but a man might wallop away at your lordship's for a fortnight."

II

I wrote all this years ago, out of what were even then old memories. I was in Roughley the other day, and found it much like other desolate places. I may have been thinking of Moughorow, a much wilder place, for the memories of one's childhood are brittle things to lean upon.

1902.

THE RELIGION OF A SAILOR

A SEA captain when he stands upon the bridge, or looks out from his deck-house, thinks much about God and about the world. Away in the valley yonder among the corn and the poppies men may well forget all things except the warmth of the sun upon the face, and the kind shadow under the hedge; but he who journeys through storm and darkness must needs think and think. One July a couple of years ago I took my supper with a Captain Moran on board the s.s. *Margaret,* that had put into a western river from I know not where. I found him a man of many notions all flavoured with his personality, as is the way with sailors. He talked in his queer sea manner of God and the world, and up through all his words broke the hard energy of his calling.

"Sur," said he, "did you ever hear tell of the sea captain's prayer?"

"No," said I; "what is it?"

"It is," he replied, " 'O Lord, give me a stiff upper lip.' "

"And what does that mean?"

"It means," he said, "that when they come to me some night and wake me up, and say, 'Captain, we're going down,' that I won't make a fool o' meself. Why, sur, we war in mid Atlantic, and I standin' on the bridge, when the third mate comes up to me lookin' mortial bad. Says he, 'Captain, all's up with us.' Says I, 'Didn't you know when you joined that a certain percentage go down every year?' 'Yes, sur,' says he; and says I, 'Arn't you paid to go down?' 'Yes, sur,' says he; and says I, 'Then go down like a man, and be damned to you!' "

CONCERNING THE NEARNESS TOGETHER OF HEAVEN, EARTH, AND PURGATORY

In Ireland this world and the world we go to after death are not far apart. I have heard of a ghost that was many years in a tree and many years in the archway of a bridge, and my old Mayo woman says, "There is a bush up at my own place, and the people do be saying that there are two souls doing their penance under it. When the wind blows one way the one has shelter, and when it blows from the north the other has the shelter. It is twisted over with the way they be rooting under it for shelter. I don't believe it, but there is many a one would not pass by it at night." Indeed there are times when the worlds are so near together that it seems as if our earthly chattels were no more than the shadows of things beyond. A lady I knew once saw a village child running about with a long trailing petticoat upon her, and asked the creature why she did not have it cut short. "It was my grandmother's," said the child; "would you have her going about yonder with her petticoat up to her knees, and she dead but four days?" I have read a story of a woman whose ghost haunted her people because they had made her grave-clothes so short that the fires of purgatory burned her knees. The peasantry expect to have beyond the grave houses much like their earthly homes, only there the thatch will never grow leaky, nor the white walls lose their lustre, nor shall the dairy be at any time empty of good milk and butter. But now and then a landlord or an agent or a gauger will go by begging his bread, to show how God divides the righteous from the unrighteous.   1892 and 1902.

THE EATERS OF PRECIOUS STONES

SOMETIMES when I have been shut off from common interests, and have for a little forgotten to be restless, I get waking dreams, now faint and shadow-like, now vivid and solid-looking, like the material world under my feet. Whether they be faint or vivid, they are ever beyond the power of my will to alter in any way. They have their own will, and sweep hither and thither, and change according to its commands. One day I saw faintly an immense pit of blackness, round which went a circular parapet, and on this parapet sat innumerable apes eating precious stones out of the palms of their hands. The stones glittered green and crimson, and the apes devoured them with an insatiable hunger. I knew that I saw the Celtic Hell, and my own Hell, the Hell of the artist, and that all who sought after beautiful and wonderful things with too avid a thirst, lost peace and form and became shapeless and common. I have seen into other people's hells also, and saw in one an infernal Peter, who had a black face and white lips, and who weighed on a curious double scales not only the evil deeds committed, but the good deeds left undone, of certain invisible shades. I could see the scales go up and down, but I could not see the shades who were, I knew, crowding about him. I saw on another occasion a quantity of demons of all kinds of shapes—fish-like, serpent-like, ape-like, and dog-like—sitting about a black pit such as that in my own Hell, and looking at a moon-like reflection of the Heavens which shone up from the depths of the pit.

OUR LADY OF THE HILLS

WHEN we were children we did not say at such a distance from the post-office, or so far from the butcher's or the grocer's, but measured things by the covered well in the wood, or by the burrow of the fox in the hill. We belonged then to God and to His works, and to things come down from the ancient days. We would not have been greatly surprised had we met the shining feet of an angel among the white mushrooms upon the mountains, for we knew in those days immense despair, unfathomed love—every eternal mood,—but now the draw-net is about our feet. A few miles eastward of Lough Gill, a young Protestant girl, who was both pretty herself and prettily dressed in blue and white, wandered up among those mountain mushrooms, and I have a letter of hers telling how she met a troop of children, and became a portion of their dream. When they first saw her they threw themselves face down in a bed of rushes, as if in a great fear; but after a little other children came about them, and they got up and followed her almost bravely. She noticed their fear, and presently stood still and held out her arms. A little girl threw herself into them with the cry, "Ah, you are the Virgin out o' the picture!" "No," said another, coming near also, "she is a sky faery, for she has the colour of the sky." "No," said a third, "she is the faery out of the foxglove grown big." The other children, however, would have it that she was indeed the Virgin, for she wore the Virgin's colours. Her good Protestant heart was greatly troubled, and she got the children to sit down about her, and tried to explain who she was, but they would have none of her explanation. Finding explanation of no avail, she asked had they ever heard of Christ? "Yes," said one; "but we do not like Him, for He would kill us if it were not for the Virgin." "Tell Him to be good to me," whispered another into her ear. "He would not let me near Him, for dad says I am a divil," burst out a third.

She talked to them a long time about Christ and the apostles, but was finally interrupted by an elderly woman with a stick, who, taking her to be some adventurous hunter for converts, drove the children away, despite their explanation that here was the great Queen of Heaven come to walk upon the mountain and be kind to them. When the children had gone she went on her way, and had walked about half-a-mile, when the child who was called "a divil" jumped down from the high ditch by the lane, and said she would believe her "an ordinary lady" if she had "two skirts," for "ladies always had two skirts." The "two skirts" were shown, and the child went away crestfallen, but a few minutes later jumped down again from the ditch, and cried angrily, "Dad's a divil, mum's a divil, and I'm a divil, and you are only an ordinary lady," and having flung a handful of mud and pebbles ran away sobbing. When my pretty Protestant had come to her own home she found that she had dropped the tassels of her parasol. A year later she was by chance upon the mountain, but wearing now a plain black dress, and met the child who had first called her the Virgin out o' the picture, and saw the tassels hanging about the child's neck, and said, "I am the lady you met last year, who told you about Christ." "No, you are not! no, you are not! no, you are not!" was the passionate reply. And after all, it was not my pretty Protestant, but Mary, Star of the Sea, still walking in sadness and in beauty upon many a mountain and by many a shore, who cast those tassels at the feet of the child. It is indeed fitting that man pray to her who is the mother of peace, the mother of dreams, and the mother of purity, to leave them yet a little hour to do good and evil in, and to watch old Time telling the rosary of the stars.

THE GOLDEN AGE

A WHILE ago I was in the train, and getting near Sligo. The last time I had been there something was troubling me, and I had longed for a message from those beings or bodiless moods, or whatever they be, who inhabit the world of spirits. The message came, for one night I saw with blinding distinctness a black animal, half weasel, half dog, moving along the top of a stone wall, and presently the black animal vanished, and from the other side came a white weasel-like dog, his pink flesh shining through his white hair and all in a blaze of light; and I remembered a pleasant belief about two faery dogs who go about representing day and night, good and evil, and was comforted by the excellent omen. But now I longed for a message of another kind, and chance, if chance there is, brought it, for a man got into the carriage and began to play on a fiddle made apparently of an old blacking-box, and though I am quite unmusical the sounds filled me with the strangest emotions. I seemed to hear a voice of lamentation out of the Golden Age. It told me that we are imperfect, incomplete, and no more like a beautiful woven web, but like a bundle of cords knotted together and flung into a corner. It said that the world was once all perfect and kindly, and that still the kindly and perfect world existed, but buried like a mass of roses under many spadefuls of earth. The faeries and the more innocent of the spirits dwelt within it, and lamented over our fallen world in the lamentation of the wind-tossed reeds, in the song of the birds, in the moan of the waves, and in the sweet cry of the fiddle. It said that with us the beautiful are not clever and the clever are not beautiful, and that the best of our moments are marred by a little vulgarity, or by a pin-prick out of sad recollection, and that the fiddle must ever lament about it all. It said that if only they who live in the Golden Age could die we might be happy, for the sad voices would be still; but alas! alas! they must sing and we must weep until the Eternal gates swing open.

We were now getting into the big glass-roofed terminus, and the fiddler put away his old blacking-box and held out his hat for a copper, and then opened the door and was gone.

A REMONSTRANCE WITH SCOTSMEN FOR HAVING SOURED THE DISPOSITION OF THEIR GHOSTS AND FAERIES

NOT only in Ireland is faery belief still extant. It was only the other day I heard of a Scottish farmer who believed that the lake in front of his house was haunted by a water-horse. He was afraid of it, and dragged the lake with nets, and then tried to pump it empty. It would have been a bad thing for the water-horse had he found him. An Irish peasant would have long since come to terms with the creature. For in Ireland there is something of timid affection between men and spirits. They only ill-treat each other in reason. Each admits the other side to have feelings. There are points beyond which neither will go. No Irish peasant would treat a captured faery as did the man Campbell tells of. He caught a kelpie, and tied her behind him on his horse. She was fierce, but he kept her quiet by driving an awl and a needle into her. They came to a river, and she grew very restless, fearing to cross the water. Again he drove the awl and needle into her. She cried out, "Pierce me with the awl, but keep that slender, hair-like slave (the needle) out of me." They came to an inn. He turned the light of a lantern on her; immediately she dropped down like a falling star, and changed into a lump of jelly. She was dead. Nor would they treat the faeries as one is treated in an old Highland poem. A faery loved a little child who used to cut turf at the side of a faery hill. Every day the faery put out his hand from the hill with an enchanted knife. The child used to cut the turf with the knife. It did not take long, the knife being charmed. Her brothers wondered why she was done so quickly. At last they resolved to watch, and find out who helped her. They saw the small hand come out of the earth, and the little child take from it the knife. When the turf was all cut, they saw her make three taps on the ground with the handle. The small hand came out of the hill. Snatching the knife from the child, they cut the hand off with a blow. The faery was never again seen. He drew his bleeding arm into the earth, thinking, as it is recorded, he had lost his hand through the treachery of the child.

In Scotland you are too theological, too gloomy. You have made even the Devil religious. "Where do you live, good-wyf, and how is the minister?" he said to the witch when he met her on the high-road, as it came out in the trial. You have burnt all the witches. In Ireland we have left them alone. To be sure, the "loyal minority" knocked out the eye of one with a cabbage-stump on the 31st of March, 1711, in the town of Carrickfergus. But then the "loyal minority" is half Scottish. You have discovered the faeries to be pagan and wicked. You would like to have them all up before the magistrate. In Ireland warlike mortals have gone amongst them, and helped them in their battles, and they in turn have taught men great skill with herbs, and permitted some few to hear their tunes. Carolan slept upon a faery rath. Ever after their tunes ran in his head, and made him the great musician he was. In Scotland you have denounced them from the pulpit. In Ireland they have been permitted by the priests to consult them on the state of their souls. Unhappily the priests have decided that they have no souls, that they will dry up like so much bright vapour at the last day; but more in sadness than in anger they have said it. The Catholic religion likes to keep on good terms with its neighbours.

These two different ways of looking at things have influenced in each country the whole world of sprites and goblins. For their gay and graceful doings you must go to Ireland; for their deeds of terror to Scotland. Our Irish faery terrors have about them something of make-believe. When a peasant strays into an enchanted hovel, and is made to turn a corpse all night on a spit before the fire, we do not feel anxious; we know he will wake in the midst of a green field, the dew on his old coat. In Scotland it is altogether different. You have soured the naturally excellent disposition of ghosts and goblins. The piper M'Crimmon, of the Hebrides, shouldered his pipes, and marched into a sea cavern, playing loudly, and followed by his dog. For a long time the people could hear the pipes. He must have gone nearly a mile, when they heard the sound of a struggle. Then the piping ceased suddenly. Some time went by, and then his dog came out of the cavern completely flayed, too weak even to howl. Nothing else ever came out of the cavern. Then there is the tale of the man who dived into a lake where treasure was thought to be. He saw a great coffer of iron. Close to the coffer lay a monster, who warned him to return whence he came. He rose to the surface; but the bystanders, when they heard he had seen the treasure, persuaded him to dive again. He dived. In a little while his heart and liver floated up, reddening the water. No man ever saw the rest of his body.

These water-goblins and water-monsters are common in Scottish folk-lore. We have them too, but take them much less dreadfully. Our tales turn all their doings to favour and to prettiness, or hopelessly humorize the creatures. A hole in the Sligo river is haunted by one of these monsters. He is ardently believed in by many, but that does not prevent the peasantry playing with the subject, and surrounding it with conscious fantasies. When I was a small boy I fished one day for congers in the monster hole. Returning home, a great eel on my shoulder, his head flapping down in front, his tail sweeping the ground behind, I met a fisherman of my acquaintance. I began a tale of an immense conger, three times larger than the one I carried, that had broken my line and escaped. "That was him," said the fisherman. "Did you ever hear how he made my brother emigrate? My brother was a diver, you know, and grubbed stones for the Harbour Board. One day the beast comes up to him, and says, 'What are you after?' 'Stones, sur,' says he. 'Don't you think you had better be going?' 'Yes, sur,' says he. And that's why my brother emigrated. The people said it was because he got poor, but that's not true."

You—you will make no terms with the spirits of fire and earth and air and water. You have made the Darkness your enemy. We—we exchange civilities with the world beyond.

WAR

WHEN there was a rumour of war with France a while ago, I met a poor Sligo woman, a soldier's widow, that I know, and I read her a sentence out of a letter I had just had from London: "The people here are mad for war, but France seems inclined to take things peacefully," or some like sentence. Her mind ran a good deal on war, which she imagined partly from what she had heard from soldiers, and partly from tradition of the rebellion of '98, but the word London doubled her interest, for she knew there were a great many people in London, and she herself had once lived in "a congested district." "There are too many over one another in London. They are getting tired of the world. It is killed they want to be. It will be no matter; but sure the French want nothing but peace and quietness. The people here don't mind the war coming. They could not be worse than they are. They may as well die soldierly before God. Sure they will get quarters in heaven." Then she began to say that it would be a hard thing to see children tossed about on bayonets, and I knew her mind was running on traditions of the great rebellion. She said presently, "I never knew a man that was in a battle that liked to speak of it after. They'd sooner be throwing hay down from a hayrick." She told me how she and her neighbours used to be sitting over the fire when she was a girl, talking of the war that was coming, and now she was afraid it was coming again, for she had dreamed that all the bay was "stranded and covered with seaweed." I asked her if it was in the Fenian times that she had been so much afraid of war coming. But she cried out, "Never had I such fun and pleasure as in the Fenian times. I was in a house where some of the officers used to be staying, and in the daytime I would be walking after the soldiers' band, and at night I'd be going down to the end of the garden watching a soldier, with his red coat on him, drilling the Fenians in the field behind the house. One night the boys tied the liver of an old horse, that had been dead three weeks, to the knocker, and I found it when I opened the door in the morning." And presently our talk of war shifted, as it had a way of doing, to the battle of the Black Pig, which seems to her a battle between Ireland and England, but to me an Armageddon which shall quench all things in the Ancestral Darkness again, and from this to sayings about war and vengeance. "Do you know," she said, "what the curse of the Four Fathers is? They put the man-child on the spear, and somebody said to them, 'You will be cursed in the fourth generation after you,' and that is why disease or anything always comes in the fourth generation."

1902.

THE QUEEN AND THE FOOL

I HAVE heard one Hearne, a witch-doctor, who is on the border of Clare and Galway, say that in "every household" of faery "there is a queen and a fool," and that if you are "touched" by either you never recover, though you may from the touch of any other in faery. He said of the fool that he was "maybe the wisest of all," and spoke of him as dressed like one of the "mummers that used to be going about the country." Since then a friend has gathered me some few stories of him, and I have heard that he is known, too, in the highlands. I remember seeing a long, lank, ragged man sitting by the hearth in the cottage of an old miller not far from where I am now writing, and being told that he was a fool; and I find from the stories that my friend has gathered that he is believed to go to faery in his sleep; but whether he becomes an *Amadán-na-Breena,* a fool of the forth, and is attached to a household there, I cannot tell. It was an old woman that I know well, and who has been in faery herself, that spoke of him. She said, "There are fools amongst them, and the fools we see, like that *Amadán* of Bally-lee, go away with them at night, and so do the woman fools that we call *Oinseachs* (apes)." A woman who is related to the witch-doctor on the border of Clare, and who can cure people and cattle by spells, said, "There are some cures I can't do. I can't help any one that has got a stroke from the queen or the fool of the forth. I knew of a woman that saw the queen one time, and she looked like any Christian. I never heard of any that saw the fool but one woman that was walking near Gort, and she called out, 'There's the fool of the forth coming after me.' So her friends that were with her called out, though they could see nothing, and I suppose he went away at that, for she got no harm. He was like a big strong man, she said, and half naked, and that is all she said about him. I have never seen any myself, but I am a cousin of Hearne, and my uncle was away twenty-one years." The wife of the old miller said, "It is said they are mostly good neighbours, but the stroke of the fool is what there is no cure for; any one that gets that is gone. The *Amadán-na-Breena* we call him!" And an old woman who lives in the Bog of Kiltartan, and is very poor, said, "It is true enough, there is no cure for the stroke of the *Amadán-na-Breena*. There was an old man I knew long ago, he had a tape, and he could tell what diseases you had with measuring you; and he knew many things. And he said to me one time, 'What month of the year is the worst?' and I said, 'The month of May, of course.' 'It is not,' he said; 'but the month of June, for that's the month that the *Amadán* gives his stroke!' They say he looks like any other man, but he's leathan (wide), and not smart. I knew a boy one time got a great fright, for a lamb looked over the wall at him with a beard on it, and he knew it was the *Amadán,* for it was the month of June. And they brought him to that man I was telling about, that had the tape, and when he saw him he said, 'Send for the priest, and get a Mass said over him.' And so they did, and what would you say but he's living yet and has a family! A certain Regan said, 'They, the other sort of people, might be passing you close here and they might touch you. But any that gets the touch of the *Amadán-na-Breena* is done for.' It's true enough that it's in the month of June he's most likely to give the touch. I knew one that got it, and he told me about it himself. He was a boy I knew well, and he told me that one night a gentleman came to him, that had been his landlord, and that was dead. And he told him to come along with him, for he wanted him to fight another man. And when he went he found two great troops of them, and the other troop had a living man with them too, and he was put to fight him. And they had a great fight, and he got the better of the other man, and then the troop on his side gave a great shout, and he was left home again. But about three years after that he was cutting bushes in a wood and he saw the *Amadán* coming at him. He had a big vessel in his arms, and it was shining, so that the boy could see nothing else; but he put it behind his back then and came running, and the boy said he looked wild and wide, like the side of the hill. And the boy ran, and he threw the vessel after him, and it broke with a great noise, and whatever came out of it, his head was gone there and then. He lived for a while after, and used to tell us many things, but his wits were gone. He thought they mightn't have liked him to beat the other man, and he used to be afraid something would come on him." And an old woman in a Galway workhouse, who had some little knowledge of Queen Maive, said the other day, "The *Amadán-na-Breena* changes his shape every two days. Sometimes he comes like a youngster, and then he'll come like the worst of beasts, trying to give the touch he used to be. I heard it said of late he was shot, but I think myself it would be hard to shoot him."

I knew a man who was trying to bring before his mind's eye an image of Ængus, the old Irish god of love and poetry and ecstasy, who changed four of his kisses into birds, and suddenly the image of a man with a cap and bells rushed before his mind's eye, and grew vivid and spoke and called itself "Ængus' messenger." And I knew another man, a truly great seer, who saw a white fool in a visionary garden, where there was a tree with peacocks' feathers instead of leaves, and flowers that opened to show little human faces when the white fool had touched them with his coxcomb, and he saw at another time a white fool sitting by a pool and smiling and watching the images of many fair women floating up from the pool.

What else can death be but the beginning of wisdom and power and beauty? and foolishness may be a kind of death. I cannot think it wonderful that many should see a fool with a shining vessel of some enchantment or wisdom or dream too powerful for mortal brains in "every household of them." It is natural, too, that there should be a queen to every household of them, and that one should hear little of their kings, for women come more easily than men to that wisdom which ancient peoples, and all wild peoples even now, think the only wisdom. The self, which is the foundation of our knowledge, is broken in pieces by foolishness, and is forgotten in the sudden emotions of women, and therefore fools may get, and women do get of a certainty, glimpses of much that sanctity finds at the end of its painful journey. The man who saw the white fool said of a certain woman, not a peasant woman, "If I had her power of vision I would know all the wisdom of the gods, and her visions do not interest her." And I know of another woman, also not a peasant woman, who would pass in sleep into countries of an unearthly beauty, and who never cared for anything but to be busy about her house and her children; and presently an herb doctor cured her, as he called it. Wisdom and beauty and power may sometimes, as I think, come to those who die every day they live, though their dying may not be like the dying Shakespeare spoke of. There is a war between the living and the dead, and the Irish stories keep harping upon it. They will have it that when the potatoes or the wheat or any other of the fruits of the earth decay, they ripen in faery, and that our dreams lose their wisdom when the sap rises in the trees, and that our dreams can make the trees wither, and that one hears the bleating of the lambs of faery in November, and that blind eyes can see more than other eyes. Because the soul always believes in these, or in like things, the cell and the wilderness shall never be long empty, or lovers come into the world who will not understand the verse—

Heardst thou not sweet words among
That heaven-resounding minstrelsy?
Heardst thou not that those who die
Awake in a world of ecstasy?
How love, when limbs are interwoven,
And sleep, when the night of life is cloven,
And thought to the world's dim boundaries clinging,

And music when one's beloved is singing,
Is death?

1901.

THE FRIENDS OF THE PEOPLE
OF FAERY

THOSE that see the people of faery most often, and so have the most of their wisdom, are often very poor, but often, too, they are thought to have a strength beyond that of man, as though one came, when one has passed the threshold of trance, to those sweet waters where Maeldun saw the dishevelled eagles bathe and become young again.

There was an old Martin Roland, who lived near a bog a little out of Gort, who saw them often from his young days, and always towards the end of his life, though I would hardly call him their friend. He told me a few months before his death that "they" would not let him sleep at night with crying things at him in Irish, and with playing their pipes. He had asked a friend of his what he should do, and the friend had told him to buy a flute, and play on it when they began to shout or to play on their pipes, and maybe they would give up annoying him; and he did, and they always went out into the field when he began to play. He showed me the pipe, and blew through it, and made a noise, but he did not know how to play; and then he showed me where he had pulled his chimney down, because one of them used to sit up on it and play on the pipes. A friend of his and mine went to see him a little time ago, for she heard that "three of them" had told him he was to die. He said they had gone away after warning him, and that the children (children they had "taken," I suppose) who used to come with them, and play about the house with them, had "gone to some other place," because "they found the house too cold for them, maybe"; and he died a week after he had said these things.

His neighbours were not certain that he really saw any-thing in his old age, but they were all certain that he saw things when he was a young man. His brother said, "Old he is, and it's all in his brain the things he sees. If he was a young man we might believe in him." But he was im-provident, and never got on with his brothers. A neighbour said, "The poor man, they say they are mostly in his head now, but sure he was a fine fresh man twenty years ago the night he saw them linked in two lots, like young slips of girls walking together. It was the night they took away Fallon's little girl." And she told how Fallon's little girl had met a woman "with red hair that was as bright as silver," who took her away. Another neighbour, who was herself "clouted over the ear" by one of them for going into a fort where they were, said, "I believe it's mostly in his head they are; and when he stood in the door last night I said, 'The wind does be always in my ears, and the sound of it never stops,' to make him think it was the same with him; but he says, 'I hear them singing and making music all the time, and one of them is after bringing out a little flute, and it's on it he's playing to them.' And this I know, that when he pulled down the chimney where he said the piper used to be sitting and playing, he lifted up stones, and he an old man, that I could not have lifted when I was young and strong."

A friend has sent me from Ulster an account of one who was on terms of true friendship with the people of faery. It has been taken down accurately, for my friend, who had heard the old woman's story some time before I heard of it, got her to tell it over again, and wrote it out at once. She began by telling the old woman that she did not like being in the house alone because of the ghosts and fairies; and the old woman said, "There's nothing to be frightened about in faeries, miss. Many's the time I talked to a woman myself that was a faery, or something of the sort, and no less and more than mortal anyhow. She used to come about your grandfather's house—your mother's grandfather, that is—in my young days. But you'll have heard all about her." My friend said that she had heard about her, but a long time before, and she wanted to hear about her again; and the old woman went on, "Well dear, the very first time ever I heard word of her coming about was when your uncle—that is, your mother's uncle—Joseph married, and building a house for his wife, for he brought her first to his father's, up at the house by the Lough. My father and us were living nigh hand to where the new house was to be built, to overlook the men at their work. My father was a weaver, and brought his looms and all there into a cottage that was close by. The foundations were marked out, and the building stones lying about, but the masons had not come yet; and one day I was standing with my mother fornent the house, when we sees a smart wee woman coming up the field over the burn to us. I was a bit of a girl at the time, playing about and sporting myself, but I mind her as well as if I saw her there now!" My friend asked how the woman was dressed, and the old woman said, "It was a gray cloak she had on, with a green cashmere skirt and a black silk handkercher tied round her head, like the country women did use to wear in them times." My friend asked, "How wee was she?" And the old woman said, "Well now, she wasn't wee at all when I think of it, for all we called her the Wee Woman. She was bigger than many a one, and yet not tall as you would say. She was like a woman about thirty, brown-haired and round in the face. She was like Miss Betty, your grandmother's sister, and Betty was like none of the rest, not like your grandmother, nor any of them. She was round and fresh in the face, and she never was married, and she never would take any man; and we used to say that the Wee Woman—her being like Betty—was, maybe, one of their own people that had been took off before she grew to her full height, and for that she was always following us and warning and foretelling. This time she walks straight over to where my mother was standing. 'Go over to the Lough this minute!' —ordering her like that—'Go over to the Lough, and tell Joseph that he must change the foundation of this house to where I'll show you fornent the thornbush. That is where it is to be built, if he is to have luck and prosperity, so do what I'm telling ye this minute.' The house was being built on 'the path' I suppose—the path used by the people of faery in their journeys, and my mother brings Joseph down and shows him, and he changes the foundations, the way he was bid, but didn't bring it exactly to where was pointed, and the end of that was, when he come to the house, his own wife lost her life with an accident that come to a horse that hadn't room to turn right with a harrow between the bush and the wall. The Wee Woman was queer and angry when next she come, and says to us, 'He didn't do as I bid him, but he'll see what he'll see.' " My friend asked where the woman came from this time, and if she was dressed as before, and the woman said, "Always the same way, up the field beyant the burn. It was a thin sort of shawl she had about her in summer, and a cloak about her in winter; and many and many a time she came, and always it was good advice she was giving to my mother, and warning her what not to do if she would have good luck. There was none of the other children of us ever seen her unless me; but I used to be glad when I seen her coming up the burn, and would run out and catch her by the hand and the cloak, and call to my mother, 'Here's the Wee Woman!' No man body ever seen her. My father used to be wanting to, and was angry with my mother and me, thinking we were telling lies and talking foolish like. And so one day when she had come, and was sitting by the fireside talking to my mother, I slips out to the field where he was digging. 'Come up,' says I, 'if ye want to see her. She's sitting at the fireside now, talking to mother.' So in he comes with me and looks round angry like and sees nothing, and he up with a broom that was near hand and hits me a crig with it. 'Take that now!' says he, 'for making a fool of me!' and away with him as fast as he could, and queer and angry with me. The Wee Woman says to me then, 'Ye got that now for bringing people to see me. No man body ever seen me, and none ever will.'

"There was one day, though, she gave him a queer fright anyway, whether he had seen her or not. He was in among the cattle when it happened, and he comes up to the house all trembling like. 'Don't let me hear you say another word of your Wee Woman. I have got enough of her this time.' Another time, all the same, he was up Gortin to sell horses, and before he went off, in steps the Wee Woman and says she to my mother, holding out a sort of a weed, 'Your man is gone up by Gortin, and there's a bad fright waiting him coming home, but take this and sew it in his coat, and he'll get no harm by it.' My mother takes the herb, but thinks to herself, 'Sure there's nothing in it,' and throws it on the floor, and lo and behold, and sure enough! coming home from Gortin, my father got as bad a fright as ever he got in his life. What it was I don't right mind, but anyway he was badly damaged by it. My mother was in a queer way, frightened of the Wee Woman, after what she done, and sure enough the next time she was angry. 'Ye didn't believe me,' she said, 'and ye threw the herb I gave ye in the fire, and I went far enough for it.' There was another time she came and told how William Hearne was dead in America. 'Go over,' she says, 'to the Lough, and say that William is dead, and he died happy, and this was the last Bible chapter ever he read,' and with that she gave the verse and chapter. 'Go,' she says, 'and tell them to read them at the next class meeting, and that I held his head while he died.' And sure enough word came after that how William had died on the day she named. And, doing as she did about the chapter and hymn, they never had such a prayer-meeting as that. One day she and me and my mother was standing talking, and she was warning her about something, when she says of a sudden, 'Here comes Miss Letty in all her finery, and it's time for me to be off.' And with that she gave a swirl round on her feet, and raises up in the air, and round and round she goes, and up and up, as if it was a winding stairs she went up, only far swifter. She went up and up, till she was no bigger than a bird up against the clouds, singing and singing the whole time the loveliest music I ever heard in my life from that day to this. It wasn't a hymn she was singing, but poetry, lovely poetry, and me and my mother stands gaping up, and all of a tremble. 'What is she at all, mother?' says I. 'Is it an angel she is, or a faery woman, or what?' With that up come Miss Letty, that was your grandmother, dear, but Miss Letty she was then, and no word of her being anything else, and she wondered to see us gaping up that way, till me and my mother told her of it. She went on gay-dressed then, and was lovely looking. She was up the lane where none of us could see her coming forward when the Wee Woman rose up in that queer way, saying, 'Here comes Miss Letty in all her finery.' Who knows to what far country she went, or to see whom dying?

"It was never after dark she came, but daylight always, as far as I mind, but wanst, and that was on a Hallow Eve night. My mother was by the fire, making ready the supper; she had a duck down and some apples. In slips the Wee Woman, 'I'm come to pass my Hallow Eve with you,' says she. 'That's right,' says my mother, and thinks to herself, 'I can give her her supper nicely.' Down she sits by the fire a while. 'Now I'll tell you where you'll bring my supper,' says she. 'In the room beyond there beside the loom—set a chair in and a plate.' 'When ye're spending the night, mayn't ye as well sit by the table and eat with the rest of us?' 'Do what you're bid, and set whatever you give me in the room beyant. I'll eat there and nowhere else.' So my mother sets her a plate of duck and some apples, whatever was going, in where she bid, and we got to our supper and she to hers; and when we rose I went in, and there, lo and behold ye, was her supper-plate a bit ate of each portion, and she clean gone!"

1897.

DREAMS THAT HAVE NO MORAL

THE friend who heard about Maive and the hazel-stick went to the workhouse another day. She found the old people cold and wretched, "like flies in winter," she said; but they forgot the cold when they began to talk. A man had just left them who had played cards in a rath with the people of faery, who had played "very fair"; and one old man had seen an enchanted black pig one night, and there were two old people my friend had heard quarrelling as to whether Raftery or Callanan was the better poet. One had said of Raftery, "He was a big man, and his songs have gone through the whole world. I remember him well. He had a voice like the wind"; but the other was certain "that you would stand in the snow to listen to Callanan." Presently an old man began to tell my friend a story, and all listened delightedly, bursting into laughter now and then. The story, which I am going to tell just as it was told, was one of those old rambling moralless tales, which are the delight of the poor and the hard driven, wherever life is left in its natural simplicity. They tell of a time when nothing had consequences, when even if you were killed, if only you had a good heart, somebody would bring you to life again with a touch of a rod, and when if you were a prince and happened to look exactly like your brother, you might go to bed with his queen, and have only a little quarrel afterwards. We too, if we were so weak and poor that everything threatened us with misfortune, would remember, if foolish people left us alone, every old dream that has been strong enough to fling the weight of the world from its shoulders.

There was a king one time who was very much put out because he had no son, and he went at last to consult his chief adviser. And the chief adviser said, "It's easy enough managed if you do as I tell you. Let you send some one," says he, "to such a place to catch a fish. And when the fish is brought in, give it to the queen, your wife, to eat."

So the king sent as he was told, and the fish was caught and brought in, and he gave it to the cook, and bade her put it before the fire, but to be careful with it, and not to let any blob or blister rise on it. But it is impossible to cook a fish before the fire without the skin of it rising in some place or other, and so there came a blob on the skin, and the cook put her finger on it to smooth it down, and then she put her finger into her mouth to cool it, and so she got a taste of the fish. And then it was sent up to the queen, and she ate it, and what was left of it was thrown out into the yard, and there was a mare in the yard and a greyhound, and they ate the bits that were thrown out.

And before a year was out, the queen had a young son, and the cook had a young son, and the mare had two foals, and the greyhound had two pups.

And the two young sons were sent out for a while to some place to be cared, and when they came back they were so much like one another no person could know which was the queen's son and which was the cook's. And the queen was vexed at that, and she went to the chief adviser and said, "Tell me some way that I can know which is my own son, for I don't like to be giving the same eating and drinking to the cook's son as to my own." "It is easy to know that," said the chief adviser, "if you will do as I tell you. Go you outside, and stand at the door they will be coming in by, and when they see you, your own son will bow his head, but the cook's son will only laugh."

So she did that, and when her own son bowed his head, her servants put a mark on him that she would know him again. And when they were all sitting at their dinner after that, she said to Jack, that was the cook's son, "It is time for you to go away out of this, for you are not my son." And her own son, that we will call Bill, said, "Do not send him away, are we not brothers?" But Jack said, "I would have been long ago out of this house if I knew it was not my own father and mother owned it." And for all Bill could say to him, he would not stop. But before he went, they were by the well that was in the garden, and he said to Bill, "If harm ever happens to me, that water on the top of the well will be blood, and the water below will be honey."

Then he took one of the pups, and one of the two horses, that was foaled after the mare eating the fish, and the wind that was after him could not catch him, and he caught the wind that was before him. And he went on till he came to a weaver's house, and he asked him for a lodging, and he gave it to him. And then he went on till he came to a king's house, and he sent in at the door to ask, "Did he want a servant?" "All I want," said the king, "is a boy that will drive out the cows to the field every morning, and bring them in at night to be milked." "I will do that for you," said Jack; so the king engaged him.

In the morning Jack was sent out with the four-and-twenty cows, and the place he was told to drive them to had not a blade of grass in it for them, but was full of stones. So Jack looked about for some place where there would be better grass, and after a while he saw a field with good green grass in it, and it belonging to a giant. So he knocked down a bit of the wall and drove them in, and he went up himself into an apple-tree and began to eat the apples. Then the giant came into the field. "Fee-faw-fum," says he, "I smell the blood of an Irishman. I see you where you are, up in the tree," he said; "you are too big for one mouthful, and too small for two mouthfuls, and I don't know what I'll do with you if I don't grind you up and make snuff for my nose." "As you are strong, be merciful," says Jack up in the tree. "Come down out of that, you little dwarf," said the giant, "or I'll tear you and the tree asunder." So Jack came down. "Would you sooner be driving red-hot knives into one another's hearts," said the giant, "or would you sooner be fighting one another on red-hot flags?" "Fighting on red-hot flags is what I'm used to at home," said Jack, "and your dirty feet will be sinking in them and my feet will be rising." So then they began the fight. The ground that was hard they made soft, and the ground that was soft they made hard, and they made spring wells come up through the green flags. They were like that all through the day, no one getting the upper hand of the other, and at last a little bird came and sat on the bush and said to Jack, "If you don't make an end of him by sunset, he'll make an end of you." Then Jack put out his strength, and he brought the giant down on his knees. "Give me my life," says the giant, "and I'll give you the three best gifts." "What are those?" said Jack. "A sword that nothing can stand against, and a suit that when you put it on, you will see everybody, and nobody will see you, and a pair of shoes that will make you run faster than the wind blows." "Where are they to be found?" said Jack. "In that red door you see there in the hill." So Jack went and got them out. "Where will I try the sword?" says he. "Try it on that ugly black stump of a tree," says the giant. "I see nothing blacker or uglier than your own head," says Jack. And with that he made one stroke, and cut off the giant's head that it went into the air, and he caught it on the sword as it was coming down, and made two halves of it. "It is well for you I did not join the body again," said the head, "or you would have never been able to strike it off again." "I did not give you the chance of that," said Jack. And he brought away the great suit with him.

So he brought the cows home at evening, and every one wondered at all the milk they gave that night. And when the king was sitting at dinner with the princess, his daughter, and the rest, he said, "I think I only hear two roars from beyond to-night in place of three."

The next morning Jack went out again with the cows,

and he saw another field full of grass, and he knocked down the wall and let the cows in. All happened the same as the day before, but the giant that came this time had two heads, and they fought together, and the little bird came and spoke to Jack as before. And when Jack had brought the giant down, he said, "Give me my life, and I'll give you the best thing I have." "What is that?" says Jack. "It's a suit that you can put on, and you will see every one but no one can see you." "Where is it?" said Jack. "It's inside that little red door at the side of the hill." So Jack went and brought out the suit. And then he cut off the giant's two heads, and caught them coming down and made four halves of them. And they said it was well for him he had not given them time to join the body.

That night when the cows came home they gave so much milk that all the vessels that could be found were filled up.

The next morning Jack went out again, and all happened as before, and the giant this time had four heads, and Jack made eight halves of them. And the giant had told him to go to a little blue door in the side of the hill, and there he got a pair of shoes that when you put them on would go faster than the wind.

That night the cows gave so much milk that there were not vessels enough to hold it, and it was given to tenants and to poor people passing the road, and the rest was thrown out at the windows. I was passing that way myself, and I got a drink of it.

That night the king said to Jack, "Why is it the cows are giving so much milk these days? Are you bringing them to any other grass?" "I am not," said Jack, "but I have a good stick, and whenever they would stop still or lie down, I give them blows of it, that they jump and leap over walls and stones and ditches; that's the way to make cows give plenty of milk."

And that night at the dinner, the king said, "I hear no roars at all."

The next morning, the king and the princess were watching at the window to see what would Jack do when he got to the field. And Jack knew they were there, and he got a stick, and began to batter the cows, that they went leaping and jumping over stones, and walls, and ditches. "There is no lie in what Jack said," said the king then.

Now there was a great serpent at that time used to come every seven years, and he had to get a king's daughter to eat, unless she would have some good man to fight for her. And it was the princess at the place Jack was had to be given to it that time, and the king had been feeding a bully underground for seven years, and you may believe he got the best of everything, to be ready to fight it.

And when the time came, the princess went out, and the bully with her down to the shore, and when they got there what did he do, but to tie the princess to a tree, the way the serpent would be able to swallow her easy with no delay, and he himself went and hid up in an ivy-tree. And Jack knew what was going on, for the princess had told him about it, and had asked would he help her, but he said he would not. But he came out now, and he put on the suit he had taken from the first giant, and he came by the place the princess was, but she didn't know him. "Is that right for a princess to be tied to a tree?" said Jack. "It is not, indeed," said she, and she told him what had happened, and how the serpent was coming to take her. "If you will let me sleep for awhile with my head in your lap," said Jack, "you could wake me when it is coming." So he did that, and she awakened him when she saw the serpent coming, and Jack got up and fought with it, and drove it back into the sea. And then he cut the rope that fastened her, and he went away. The bully came down then out of the tree, and he brought the princess to where the king was, and he said, "I got a friend of mine to come and fight the serpent to-day, where I was a little timorous after being so long shut up underground, but I'll do the fighting myself to-morrow."

The next day they went out again, and the same thing happened, the bully tied up the princess where the serpent could come at her fair and easy, and went up himself to hide in the ivy-tree. Then Jack put on the suit he had taken from the second giant, and he walked out, and the princess did not know him, but she told him all that had happened yesterday, and how some young gentleman she did not know had come and saved her. So Jack asked might he lie down and take a sleep with his head in her lap, the way she could awake him. And all happened the same way as the day before. And the bully gave her up to the king, and said he had brought another of his friends to fight for her that day.

The next day she was brought down to the shore as before, and a great many people gathered to see the serpent that was coming to bring the king's daughter away. And Jack brought out the suit of clothes he had brought away from the third giant, and she did not know him, and they talked as before. But when he was asleep this time, she thought she would make sure of being able to find him again, and she took out her scissors and cut off a piece of his hair, and made a little packet of it and put it away. And she did another thing, she took off one of the shoes that was on his feet.

And when she saw the serpent coming she woke him, and he said, "This time I will put the serpent in a way that he will eat no more king's daughters." So he took out the sword he had got from the giant, and he put it in at the back of the serpent's neck, the way blood and water came spouting out that went for fifty miles inland, and made an end of him. And then he made off, and no one saw what way he went, and the bully brought the princess to the king, and claimed to have saved her, and it is he who was made much of, and was the right-hand man after that.

But when the feast was made ready for the wedding, the princess took out the bit of hair she had, and she said she would marry no one but the man whose hair would match that, and she showed the shoe and said that she would marry no one whose foot would not fit that shoe as well. And the bully tried to put on the shoe, but so much as his toe would not go into it, and as to his hair, it didn't match at all to the bit of hair she had cut from the man that saved her.

So then the king gave a great ball, to bring all the chief men of the country together to try would the shoe fit any of them. And they were all going to carpenters and joiners getting bits of their feet cut off to try could they wear the shoe, but it was no use, not one of them could get it on.

Then the king went to his chief adviser and asked what could he do. And the chief adviser bade him to give another ball, and this time he said, "Give it to poor as well as rich."

So the ball was given, and many came flocking to it, but

the shoe would not fit any one of them. And the chief adviser said, "Is every one here that belongs to the house?"
"They are all here," said the king, "except the boy that
minds the cows, and I would not like him to be coming up
here."

Jack was below in the yard at the time, and he heard
what the king said, and he was very angry, and he went
and got his sword and came running up the stairs to strike
off the king's head, but the man that kept the gate met him
on the stairs before he could get to the king, and quieted
him down, and when he got to the top of the stairs and the
princess saw him, she gave a cry and ran into his arms.
And they tried the shoe and it fitted him, and his hair
matched to the piece that had been cut off. So then they
were married, and a great feast was given for three days
and three nights.

And at the end of that time, one morning there came a
deer outside the window, with bells on it, and they ringing.
And it called out, "Here is the hunt, where is the huntsman
and the hound?" So when Jack heard that he got up and
took his horse and his hound and went hunting the deer.
When it was in the hollow he was on the hill, and when it
was on the hill he was in the hollow, and that went on all
through the day, and when night fell it went into a wood.
And Jack went into the wood after it, and all he could see
was a mud-wall cabin, and he went in, and there he saw
an old woman, about two hundred years old, and she sitting over the fire. "Did you see a deer pass this way?" says
Jack. "I did not," says she, "but it's too late now for you
to be following a deer, let you stop the night here." "What
will I do with my horse and my hound?" said Jack. "Here
are two ribs of hair," says she, "and let you tie them up
with them." So Jack went out and tied up the horse and
the hound, and when he came in again the old woman said,
"You killed my three sons, and I'm going to kill you now,"
and she put on a pair of boxing-gloves, each one of them
nine stone weight, and the nails in them fifteen inches long.
Then they began to fight, and Jack was getting the worst
of it. "Help, hound!" he cried out, then "Squeeze hair,"
cried out the old woman, and the rib of hair that was about
the hound's neck squeezed him to death. "Help, horse!"
Jack called out, then, "Squeeze hair," called out the old

woman, and the rib of hair that was about the horse's neck began to tighten and squeeze him to death. Then the old woman made an end of Jack and threw him outside the door.

To go back now to Bill. He was out in the garden one day, and he took a look at the well, and what did he see but the water at the top was blood, and what was underneath was honey. So he went into the house again, and he said to his mother, "I will never eat a second meal at the same table, or sleep a second night in the same bed, till I know what is happening to Jack."

So he took the other horse and hound then, and set off, over the hills where cock never crows and horn never sounds, and the devil never blows his bugle. And at last he came to the weaver's house, and when he went in, the weaver says, "You are welcome, and I can give you better treatment than I did the last time you came in to me," for she thought it was Jack who was there, they were so much like one another. "That is good," said Bill to himself, "my brother has been here." And he gave the weaver the full of a basin of gold in the morning before he left.

Then he went on till he came to the king's house, and when he was at the door the princess came running down the stairs, and said, "Welcome to you back again." And all the people said, "It is a wonder you have gone hunting three days after your marriage, and to stop so long away." So he stopped that night with the princess, and she thought it was her own husband all the time.

And in the morning the deer came, and bells ringing on her, under the windows, and called out, "The hunt is here, where are the huntsmen and the hounds?" Then Bill got up and got his horse and his hound, and followed her over hills and hollows till they came to the wood, and there he saw nothing but the mud-wall cabin and the old woman sitting by the fire, and she bade him stop the night there, and gave him two ribs of hair to tie his horse and his hound with. But Bill was wittier than Jack was, and before he went out, he threw the ribs of hair into the fire secretly. When he came in the old woman said, "Your brother killed my three sons, and I killed him, and I'll kill you along with him." And she put her gloves on, and they began the fight, and then Bill called out, "Help, horse."

"Squeeze hair," called the old woman; "I can't squeeze, I'm in the fire," said the hair. And the horse came in and gave her a blow of his hoof. "Help, hound," said Bill then. "Squeeze, hair," said the old woman; "I can't, I'm in the fire," said the second hair. Then the hound put his teeth in her, and Bill brought her down, and she cried for mercy. "Give me my life," she said, "and I'll tell you where you'll get your brother again, and his hound and horse." "Where's that?" said Bill. "Do you see that rod over the fire?" said she; "take it down and go outside the door where you'll see three green stones, and strike them with the rod, for they are your brother, and his horse and hound, and they'll come to life again." "I will, but I'll make a green stone of you first," said Bill, and he cut off her head with his sword.

Then he went out and struck the stones, and sure enough there were Jack, and his horse and hound, alive and well. And they began striking other stones around, and men came from them, that had been turned to stones, hundreds and thousands of them.

Then they set out for home, but on the way they had some dispute or some argument together, for Jack was not well pleased to hear he had spent the night with his wife, and Bill got angry, and he struck Jack with the rod, and turned him to a green stone. And he went home, but the princess saw he had something on his mind, and he said then, "I have killed my brother." And he went back then and brought him to life, and they lived happy ever after, and they had children by the basketful, and threw them out by the shovelful. I was passing one time myself, and they called me in and gave me a cup of tea.   1902.

BY THE ROADSIDE

LAST night I went to a wide place on the Kiltartan road
to listen to some Irish songs. While I waited for the singers
an old man sang about that country beauty who died so
many years ago, and spoke of a singer he had known who
sang so beautifully that no horse would pass him, but must
turn its head and cock its ears to listen. Presently a score
of men and boys and girls, with shawls over their heads,
gathered under the trees to listen. Somebody sang *Sa
Muirnín Díles,* and then somebody else *Jimmy Mo
Mílestór,* mournful songs of separation, of death, and of
exile. Then some of the men stood up and began to dance,
while another lilted the measure they danced to, and then
somebody sang *Eiblín a Rúin,* that glad song of meeting
which has always moved me more than other songs, because the lover who made it sang it to his sweetheart under
the shadow of a mountain I looked at every day through
my childhood. The voices melted into the twilight and
were mixed into the trees, and when I thought of the words
they too melted away, and were mixed with the generations
of men. Now it was a phrase, now it was an attitude of
mind, an emotional form, that had carried my memory to
older verses, or even to forgotten mythologies. I was carried so far that it was as though I came to one of the four
rivers, and followed it under the wall of Paradise to the
roots of the trees of knowledge and of life. There is no song
or story handed down among the cottages that has not
words and thoughts to carry one as far, for though one can
know but a little of their ascent, one knows that they
ascend like medieval genealogies through unbroken dig-
nities to the beginning of the world. Folk art is, indeed, the
oldest of the aristocracies of thought, and because it re-
fuses what is passing and trivial, the merely clever and
pretty, as certainly as the vulgar and insincere, and because
it has gathered into itself the simplest and most unforget-
able thoughts of the generations, it is the soil where all
great art is rooted. Wherever it is spoken by the fireside,
or sung by the roadside, or carved upon the lintel, apprecia-

tion of the arts that a single mind gives unity and design to, spreads quickly when its hour is come.

In a society that has cast out imaginative tradition, only a few people—three or four thousand out of millions—favoured by their own characters and by happy circumstance, and only then after much labour, have understanding of imaginative things, and yet "the imagination is the man himself." The churches in the Middle Age won all the arts into their service because men understood that when imagination is impoverished, a principal voice—some would say the only voice—for the awakening of wise hope and durable faith, and understanding charity, can speak but in broken words, if it does not fall silent. And so it has always seemed to me that we, who would re-awaken imaginative tradition by making old songs live again, or by gathering old stories into books, take part in the quarrel of Galilee. Those who are Irish and would spread foreign ways, which, for all but a few, are ways of spiritual poverty, take part also. Their part is with those who were of Jewry, and yet cried out, "If thou let this man go thou art not Caesar's friend."

1901.

INTO THE TWILIGHT

Out-worn heart, in a time out-worn,
Come clear of the nets of wrong and right;
Laugh, heart, again in the gray twilight;
Sigh, heart, again in the dew of the morn.
Thy mother Eire is always young,
Dew ever shining and twilight gray;
Though hope fall from thee or love decay
Burning in fires of a slanderous tongue.
Come, heart, where hill is heaped upon hill,
For there the mystical brotherhood
Of hollow wood and the hilly wood
And the changing moon work out their will.
And God stands winding his lonely horn;
And Time and World are ever in flight,
And love is less kind than the gray twilight,
And hope is less dear than the dew of the morn.

THE POEMS

MISERRIMUS

There was a man whom Sorrow named his friend,
And he, of his high kinsman Sorrow dreaming,
Went walking with slow steps along the gleaming
And humming sands, where windy surges wend—
He called aloud to all the stars to lend
Their hearing, and some comfort give, but they
Among themselves laugh on and sing alway—
Then cried the man whom Sorrow named his friend:
"Oh sea, old sea, hear thou my piteous story";
The sea swept on and cried her old cry still,
Rolling along in dreams from hill to hill;
And from the persecution of her glory
He fled, and in a far-off valley stopping,
Cried all his story to the dewdrops glistening;
But naught they heard, for they are ever listening,
The dew drops, for the sound of their own dropping—
And then the man whom Sorrow named his friend
Sought once again the shore, and chose a shell
And thought, "to this will I my story tell,
And my own words re-echoing shall send
Their sadness through the hollows of its heart,
And mine own tale again for me shall sing,

And mine own whispering words be comforting
And lo—my heavy burthen may depart";
Then sang he softly nigh the pearly rim;
But the sad dweller by the seaways lone
Changed all his words to inarticulate moan
Within her wildering whirls—forgetting him.

VOICES

What do you weave so soft and bright?
The cloak I weave of sorrow;
O lovely to see in all men's sight
Shall be the cloak of sorrow—
In all men's sight.

What do you build with sails for flight?
A boat I build for sorrow:
O swift on the seas all day and night
Saileth the rover sorrow—
All day and night.

What do you weave with wool so white?
The sandals these of sorrow;
Soundless shall be the footfall light
In each man's ears of sorrow—
Sudden and light.

THE INDIAN UPON GOD

I passed along the water's edge below the humid trees,
My spirit rocked in evening light, the rushes round my
      knees,

My spirit rocked in sleep and sighs; and saw the moorfowl
    pace
All dripping on a grassy slope, and saw them cease to
    chase
Each other round in circles, and heard the eldest speak:
Who holds the world between His bill and made us strong
    or weak
Is an undying moorfowl, and He lives beyond the sky.
The rains are from His dripping wing, the moonbeams from
    His eye.
I passed a little further on and heard a lotus talk:
Who made the world and ruleth it, He hangeth on a stalk,
For I am in His image made, and all this tinkling tide
Is but a sliding drop of rain between His petals wide.
A little way within the gloom a roebuck raised his eyes
Brimful of starlight, and he said: *The Stamper of the*
    Skies,
He is a gentle roebuck; for how else, I pray, could He
Conceive a thing so sad and soft, a gentle thing like me?
I passed a little further on and heard a peacock say:
Who made the grass and made the worms and made my
    feathers gay,
He is a monstrous peacock, and He waveth all the night
His languid tail above us, lit with myriad spots of light.

THE INDIAN TO HIS LOVE

The island dreams under the dawn
And great boughs drop tranquillity;
The peahens dance on a smooth lawn,
A parrot sways upon a tree,
Raging at his own image in the dim enamelled sea.

Here we will moor our lonely ship
And wander ever with woven hands,
Murmuring softly lip to lip,
Along the grass, along the sands,
Murmuring gently how far off are the unquiet lands:

How we alone of mortals are
Hid under quiet boughs apart,
While our love grows an Indian star,
A meteor of the burning heart,
One with the glimmering tide, the wings that glimmer and
　　gleam and dart,

The great boughs, and the burnished dove
That moans and sighs a hundred days:
How when we die our shades will rove,
Where eve has hushed the feathered ways,
And drop a vapoury footfall in the tide's drowsy blaze.

THE STOLEN CHILD

Where dips the rocky highland
Of Slewth Wood in the lake,
There lies a leafy island
Where flapping herons wake
The drowsy water rats;
There we've hid our fairy vats.
Full of berries,
And of reddest stolen cherries.
Come away, O human child!
To the woods and waters wild
With a fairy, hand in hand,
For the world's more full of weeping than you can
　　understand.

Where the wave of moonlight glosses
The dim grey sands with light,
Far off by furthest Rosses
We foot it all the night,
Weaving olden dances,
Mingling hands and mingling glances
Till the moon has taken flight;
To and fro we leap

And chase the frothy bubbles
While the world is full of troubles
And is anxious in its sleep.
Come away, O human child!
To the woods and waters wild
With a fairy, hand in hand,
For the world's more full of weeping than you can
    understand.

Where the wandering water gushes
From the hills above Glen-Car,
In pools among the rushes
That scarce could bathe a star,
We seek for slumbering trout
And whispering in their ears
We give them evil dreams,
Leaning softly out
From ferns that drop their tears
Of dew on the young streams.
Come, O human child!
To the woods and waters wild
With a fairy, hand in hand,
For the world's more full of weeping than you can
    understand.

Away with us he's going,
The solemn-eyed—
He'll hear no more the lowing
Of the calves on the warm hill side,
Or the kettle on the hob
Sing peace into his breast,
Or see the brown mice bob
Round and round the oatmeal chest.
For he comes, the human child,
To the woods and waters wild
With a fairy, hand in hand,
For the world's more full of weeping than he can
    understand.

TO AN ISLE IN THE WATER

Shy one, shy one,
Shy one of my heart,
She moves in the firelight
Pensively apart.

She carries in the dishes,
And lays them in a row.
To an isle in the water
With her would I go.

She carries in the candles,
And lights the curtained room,
Shy in the doorway
And shy in the gloom;

And shy as a rabbit,
Helpful and shy.
To an isle in the water
With her would I fly.

DOWN BY THE SALLEY GARDENS

Down by the salley gardens my love and I did meet;
She passed the salley gardens with little snow-white feet.
She bid me take love easy, as the leaves grow on the tree;
But I, being young and foolish, with her would not agree.

In a field by the river my love and I did stand,
And on my leaning shoulder she laid her snow-white hand.
She bid me take life easy, as the grass grows on the weirs;
But I was young and foolish, and now am full of tears.

THE MEDITATION OF THE OLD FISHERMAN

You waves, though you dance by my feet like children
    at play,
Though you glow and you glance, though you purr and
    you dart;
In the Junes that were warmer than these are, the waves
    were more gay,
When I was a boy with never a crack in my heart.

The herring are not in the tides as they were of old;
My sorrow! for many a creak gave the creel in the cart
That carried the take to Sligo town to be sold,
When I was a boy with never a crack in my heart.

And ah, you proud maiden, you are not so fair when
    his oar
Is heard on the water, as they were, the proud and apart,
Who paced in the eve by the nets on the pebbly shore,
When I was a boy with never a crack in my heart.

THE BALLAD OF FATHER O'HART

Good Father John O'Hart
In penal days rode out
To a shoneen who had free lands
And his own snipe and trout.

In trust took he John's lands;
Sleiveens were all his race;
And he gave them as dowers to his daughters,
And they married beyond their place.

But Father John went up,
And Father John went down;
And he wore small holes in his shoes,
And he wore large holes in his gown.

All loved him, only the shoneen,
Whom the devils have by the hair,
From the wives, and the cats, and the children,
To the birds in the white of the air.

The birds, for he opened their cages
As he went up and down;
And he said with a smile, "Have peace now";
And he went his way with a frown.

But if when any one died
Came keeners hoarser than rooks,
He bade them give over their keening;
For he was a man of books.

And these were the works of John,
When weeping score by score,
People came into Coloony;
For he'd died at ninety-four.

There was no human keening;
The birds from Knocknarea
And the world round Knocknashee
Came keening in that day.

The young birds and old birds
Came flying, heavy, and sad;
Keening in from Tiraragh,
Keening from Ballinafad;

Keening from Inishmurray,
Nor stayed for bite or sup;
This way were all reproved,
Who dig old customs up.

THE BALLAD OF MOLL MAGEE

Come round me, little childer;
There, don't fling stones at me
Because I mutter as I go;
But pity Moll Magee.

My man was a poor fisher
With shore lines in the say;
My work was saltin' herrings
The whole of the long day.

And sometimes from the saltin' shed,
I scarce could drag my feet
Under the blessed moonlight,
Along the pebbly street.

I'd always been but weakly,
And my baby was just born;
A neighbour minded her by day,
I minded her till morn.

I lay upon my baby;
Ye little childer dear,
I looked on my cold baby
When the morn grew frosty and clear.

A weary woman sleeps so hard!
My man grew red and pale,
And gave me money, and bade me go
To my own place, Kinsale.

He drove me out and shut the door,
And gave his curse to me;
I went away in silence,
No neighbour could I see.

The windows and the doors were shut,
One star shone faint and green;
The little straws were turnin' round
Across the bare boreen.

I went away in silence:
Beyond old Martin's byre
I saw a kindly neighbour
Blowin' her mornin' fire.

She drew from me my story—
My money's all used up,
And still, with pityin', scornin' eye,
She gives me bite and sup.

She says my man will surely come,
And fetch me home agin;
But always, as I'm movin' round,
Without doors or within,

Pilin' the wood or pilin' the turf,
Or goin' to the well,
I'm thinkin' of my baby
And keenin' to mysel'.

And sometimes I am sure she knows
When, openin' wide His door,
God lights the stars, His candles,
And looks upon the poor.

So now, ye little childer,
Ye won't fling stones at me;
But gather with your shinin' looks
And pity Moll Magee.

THE WANDERINGS OF OISIN

BOOK I

S. Patric. You who are bent, and bald, and blind,
With a heavy heart and a wandering mind,
Have known three centuries, poets sing,

Of dalliance with a demon thing.

   OISIN. Sad to remember, sick with years,
The swift innumerable spears,
The horsemen with their floating hair,
And bowls of barley, honey, and wine,
And feet of maidens dancing in tune,
And the white body that lay by mine;
But the tale, though words be lighter than air,
Must live to be old like the wandering moon.
Caolte, and Conan, and Finn were there,
When we followed a deer with our baying hounds,
With Bran, Sgeolan, and Lomair,
And passing the Firbolgs' burial mounds,
Came to the cairn-heaped grassy hill
Where passionate Maive is stony still;
And found on the dove-gray edge of the sea
A pearl-pale, high-born lady, who rode
On a horse with bridle of findrinny;
And like a sunset were her lips,
A stormy sunset on doomed ships;
A citron colour gloomed in her hair,
But down to her feet white vesture flowed,
And with the glimmering crimson glowed
Of many a figured embroidery;
And it was bound with a pearl-pale shell
That wavered like the summer streams,
As her soft bosom rose and fell.
   S. PATRIC. You are still wrecked among heathen dreams.
   OISIN. "Why do you wind no horn?" she said.
"And every hero droop his head?
The hornless deer is not more sad
That many a peaceful moment had,
More sleek than any granary mouse,
In his own leafy forest house
Among the waving fields of fern:
The hunting of heroes should be glad."

"O pleasant maiden," answered Finn,
"We think on Oscar's pencilled urn,
And on the heroes lying slain,
On Gavra's raven-covered plain;
But where are your noble kith and kin,

And into what country do you ride?"

"My father and my mother are
Aengus and Adene, and my name
Is Niam, and my land where tide
And sleep drown sun and moon and star."

"What dream came with you that you came
To this dim shore on foam wet feet?
Did your companion wander away
From where the birds of Aengus wing?"

She said, with laughter tender and sweet:
"I have not yet, war-weary king,
Been spoken of with any one,
For love of Oisin foam wet feet
Have borne me where the tempests blind
Your mortal shores till time is done!"

"How comes it, princess, that your mind
Among undying people has run
On this young man, Oisin, my son?"

"I loved no man, though canns besought
And many a man of lofty name,
Until the Danaan poets came,
Bringing me honeyed, wandering thought
Of noble Oisin and his fame,
Of battles broken by his hands,
Of stories builded by his words
That are like coloured Asian birds
At evening in their rainless lands."

O Patric, by your brazen bell,
There was no limb of mine but fell
Into a desperate gulph of love!
"You only will I wed," I cried,
"And I will make a thousand songs,
And set your name all names above,
And captives bound with leathern thongs
Shall kneel and praise you, one by one,
At evening in my western dun."

"O Oisin, mount by me and ride
To shores by the wash of the tremulous tide,
Where men have heaped no burial mounds,
And the days pass by like a wayward tune,
Where broken faith has never been known,
And the blushes of first love never have flown;
And there I will give you a hundred hounds;
No mightier creatures bay at the moon;
And a hundred robes of murmuring silk,
And a hundred calves and a hundred sheep
Whose long wool whiter than sea froth flows,
And a hundred spears and a hundred bows,
And oil and wine and honey and milk,
And always never-anxious sleep;
While a hundred youths, mighty of limb,
But knowing nor tumult nor hate nor strife,
And a hundred maidens, merry as birds,
Who when they dance to a fitful measure
Have a speed like the speed of the salmon herds
Shall follow your horn and obey your whim,
And you shall know the Danaan leisure:
And Niam be with you for a wife."
Then she sighed gently, "It grows late,
Music and love and sleep await,
Where I would be when the white moon climbs,
The red sun falls, and the world grows dim."

And then I mounted and she bound me
With her triumphing arms around me,
And whispering to herself enwound me;
But when the horse had felt my weight,
He shook himself and neighed three times:
Caolte, Conan, and Finn came near,
And wept, and raised their lamenting hands,
And bid me stay, with many a tear;
But we rode out from the human lands.

In what far kingdom do you go,
Ah, Fenians, with the shield and bow?
Or are you phantoms white as snow,
Whose lips had life's most prosperous glow?
O you, with whom in sloping valleys,

Or down the dewy forest alleys,
I chased at morn the flying deer,
With whom I hurled the hurrying spear,
And heard the foemen's bucklers rattle,
And broke the heaving ranks of battle!
And Bran, Sgeolan, and Lomair,
Where are you with your long rough hair?
You go not where the red deer feeds,
Nor tear the foemen from their steeds.

   S. PATRIC. Boast not, nor mourn with drooping head
Companions long accurst and dead.
And hounds for centuries dust and air.

   OISIN. We galloped over the glossy sea:
I know not if days passed or hours,
And Niam sang continually
Danaan songs, and their dewy showers
Of pensive laughter, unhuman sound,
Lulled weariness, and softly round
My human sorrow her white arms wound.

On! on! and now a hornless deer
Passed by us, chased by a phantom hound
All pearly white, save one red ear;
And now a maiden rode like the wind
With an apple of gold in her tossing hand,
And with quenchless eyes and fluttering hair
A beautiful young man followed behind.

"Were these two born in the Danaan land,
Or have they breathed the mortal air?"
"Vex them no longer," Niam said,
And sighing bowed her gentle head,
And sighing laid the pearly tip
Of one long finger on my lip.

But now the moon like a white rose shone
In the pale west, and the sun's rim sank,
And clouds arrayed their rank on rank
About his fading crimson ball:
The floor of Emen's hosting hall
Was not more level than the sea,
As full of loving phantasy,

And with low murmurs we rode on,
Where many a trumpet-twisted shell
That in immortal silence sleeps
Dreaming of her own melting hues,
Her golds, her ambers, and her blues,
Pierced with soft light the shallowing deeps
But now a wandering land breeze came
And a far sound of feathery quires;
It seemed to blow from the dying flame,
They seemed to sing in the smouldering fires.
The horse towards the music raced,
Neighing along the lifeless waste;
Like sooty fingers, many a tree
Rose ever out of the warm sea;
And they were trembling ceaselessly,
As though they all were beating time,
Upon the centre of the sun,
To that low laughing woodland rhyme.
And, now our wandering hours were done,
We cantered to the shore, and knew
The reason of the trembling trees:
Round every branch the song-birds flew,
Or clung thereon like swarming bees;
While round the shore a million stood
Like drops of frozen rainbow light,
And pondered in a soft vain mood,
Upon their shadows in the tide,
And told the purple deeps their pride,
And murmured snatches of delight;
And on the shores were many boats
With bending sterns and bending bows,
And carven figures on their prows
Of bitterns, and fish-eating stoats,
And swans with their exultant throats:
And where the wood and waters meet
We tied the horse in a leafy clump,
And Niam blew three merry notes
Out of a little silver trump;
And then an answering whisper flew
Over the bare and woody land,
A whisper of impetuous feet,
And ever nearer, nearer grew;

And from the woods rushed out a band
Of men and maidens, hand in hand,
And singing, singing altogether;
Their brows were white as fragrant milk,
Their cloaks made out of yellow silk,
And trimmed with many a crimson feather:
And when they saw the cloak I wore
Was dim with mire of a mortal shore,
They fingered it and gazed on me
And laughed like murmurs of the sea;
But Niam with a swift distress
Bid them away and hold their peace;
And when they heard her voice they ran
And knelt them, every maid and man,
And kissed, as they would never cease,
Her pearl-pale hand and the hem of her dress,
She bade them bring us to the hall
Where Aengus dreams, from sun to sun,
A Druid dream of the end of days
When the stars are to wane and the world be done.

They led us by long and shadowy ways
Where drops of dew in myriads fall,
And tangled creepers every hour
Blossom in some new crimson flower,
And once a sudden laughter sprang
From all their lips, and once they sang
Together, while the dark woods rang,
And made in all their distant parts,
With boom of bees in honey marts,
A rumour of delighted hearts.
And once a maiden by my side
Gave me a harp, and bid me sing,
And touch the laughing silver string;
But when I sang of human joy
A sorrow wrapped each merry face,
And, Patric! by your beard, they wept,
Until one came, a tearful boy;
"A sadder creature never stept
Than this strange human bard," he cried;
And caught the silver harp away,
And, weeping over the white strings, hurled

It down in a leaf-hid, hollow place
That kept dim waters from the sky;
And each one said with a long, long sigh,
"O saddest harp in all the world,
Sleep there till the moon and the stars die!"

And now still sad we came to where
A beautiful young man dreamed within
A house of wattles, clay, and skin;
One hand upheld his beardless chin,
And one a sceptre flashing out
Wild flames of red and gold and blue,
Like to a merry wandering rout
Of dancers leaping in the air,
And men and maidens knelt them there
And showed their eyes with teardrops dim,
And with low murmurs prayed to him,
And kissed the sceptre with red lips,
And touched it with their finger-tips.

He held that flashing sceptre up.
"Joy drowns the twilight in the dew,
And fills with stars night's purple cup,
And wakes the sluggard seeds of corn,
And stirs the young kid's budding horn,
And makes the infant ferns unwrap,
And for the peewit paints his cap,
And rolls along the unwieldly sun,
And makes the little planets run:
And if joy were not on the earth,
There were an end of change and birth,
And earth and heaven and hell would die,
And in some gloomy barrow lie
Folded like a frozen fly;
Then mock at Death and Time with glances
And wavering arms and wandering dances.

"Men's hearts of old were drops of flame
That from the saffron morning came,
Or drops of silver joy that fell
Out of the moon's pale twisted shell;
But now hearts cry that hearts are slaves,

And toss and turn in narrow caves;
But here there is nor law nor rule,
Nor have hands held a weary tool;
And here there is nor Change nor Death,
But only kind and merry breath,
For joy is God and God is joy."
With one long glance on maid and boy
And the pale blossom of the moon,
He fell into a Druid swoon.

And in a wild and sudden dance
We mocked at Time and Fate and Chance,
And swept out of the wattled hall
And came to where the dewdrops fall
Among the foamdrops of the sea,
And there we hushed the revelry;
And, gathering on our brows a frown,
Bent all our swaying bodies down,
And to the waves that glimmer by
That slooping green De Danaan sod
Sang, "God is joy and joy is God,
And things that have grown sad are wicked,
And things that fear the dawn of the morrow,
Or the gray wandering osprey Sorrow."

We danced to where in the winding thicket
The damask roses, bloom on bloom,
Like crimson meteors hang in the gloom
And bending over them softly said,
Bending over them in the dance
With a swift and friendly glance
From dewy eyes: "Upon the dead
Fall the leaves of other roses,
On the dead dim earth encloses:
But never, never on our graves,
Heaped beside the glimmering waves,
Shall fall the leaves of damask roses.
For neither Death nor Change comes near us,
And all listless hours fear us,
And we fear no dawning morrow,
Nor the gray wandering osprey Sorrow."

The dance wound through the windless woods;
The ever-summered solitudes;
Until the tossing arms grew still
Upon the woody central hill;
And, gathered in a panting band,
We flung on high each waving hand,
And sang unto the starry broods:
In our raised eyes there flashed a glow
Of milky brightness to and fro
As thus our song arose: "You stars,
Across your wandering ruby cars
Shake the loose reins: you slaves of God
He rules you with an iron rod,
He holds you with an iron bond,
Each one woven to the other,
Each one woven to his brother
Like bubbles in a frozen pond;
But we in a lonely land abide
Unchainable as the dim tide,
With hearts that know nor law nor rule,
And hands that hold no wearisome tool
Folded in love that fears no morrow,
Nor the gray wandering osprey Sorrow."
O Patric! for a hundred years
I chased upon that woody shore
The deer, the badger, and the boar.

O Patric! for a hundred years
At evening on the glimmering sands,
Beside the piled-up hunting spears,
These now outworn and withered hands
Wrestled among the island bands.
O Patric! for a hundred years
We went a-fishing in long boats
With bending sterns and bending bows,
And carven figures on their prows
Of bitterns and fish-eating stoats.
O Patric! for a hundred years
The gentle Niam was my wife;
But now two things devour my life;
The things that most of all I hate;
Fasting and prayers.

S. PATRIC.   Tell on.
    OISIN.   Yes, yes,
For these were ancient Oisin's fate
Loosed long ago from heaven's gate,
For his last days to lie in wait.

When one day by the shore I stood,
I drew out of the numberless
White flowers of the foam a staff of wood
From some dead warrior's broken lance:
I turned it in my hands; the stains
Of war were on it, and I wept,
Remembering how the Fenians stept
Along the blood-bedabbled plains,
Equal to good or grievous chance:
Thereon young Niam softly came
And caught my hands, but spake no word
Save only many times my name,
In murmurs, like a frighted bird.
We passed by woods, and lawns of clover,
And found the horse and bridled him,
For we knew well the old was over.
I heard one say "his eyes grow dim
With all the ancient sorrow of men."
And wrapped in dreams rode out again
With hoofs of the pale findrinny
Over the glimmering purple sea:
Under the golden evening light.
The immortals moved among the fountains
By rivers and the woods' old night;
Some danced like shadows on the mountains
Some wandered ever hand in hand,
Or sat in dreams on the pale strand;
Each forehead like an obscure star
Bent down above each hooked knee:
And sang, and with a dreamy gaze
Watched where the sun in a saffron blaze
Was slumbering half in the sea ways;
And, as they sang, the painted birds
Kept time with their bright wings and feet;
Like drops of honey came their words,
But fainter than a young lamb's bleat.

"An old man stirs the fire to a blaze,
In the house of a child, of a friend, of a brother;
He has over-lingered his welcome; the days,
Grown desolate, whisper and sigh to each other;
He hears the storm in the chimney above,
And bends to the fire and shakes with the cold,
While his heart still dreams of battle and love,
And the cry of the hounds on the hills of old.

"But we are apart in the grassy places,
Where care cannot trouble the least of our days,
Or the softness of youth be gone from our faces,
Or love's first tenderness die in our gaze.
The hare grows old as she plays in the sun
And gazes around her with eyes of brightness;
Before the swift things that she dreamed of were done
She limps along in an aged whiteness;
A storm of birds in the Asian trees
Like tulips in the air a-winging,
And the gentle waves of the summer seas,
That raise their heads and wander singing,
Must murmur at last 'unjust, unjust'
And 'my speed is a weariness,' falters the mouse;
And the kingfisher turns to a ball of dust,
And the roof falls in of his tunnelled house.
But the love-dew dims our eyes till the day
When God shall come from the sea with a sigh
And bid the stars drop down from the sky,
And the moon like a pale rose wither away."

BOOK II

Now, man of croziers, shadows called our names
And then away, away, like whirling flames;
And now fled by, mist-covered, without sound,
The youth and lady and the deer and hound;
"Gaze no more on the phantoms," Niam said,
And kissed my eyes, and, swaying her bright head
And her bright body, sang of faery and man

Before God was or my old line began;
Wars shadowy, vast, exultant; faeries of old
Who wedded men with rings of Druid gold;
And how those lovers never turn their eyes
Upon the life that fades and flickers and dies,
But love and kiss on dim shores far away
Rolled round with music of the sighing spray:
But sang no more, as when, like a brown bee
That has drunk full, she crossed the misty sea
With me in her white arms a hundred years
Before this day; for now the fall of tears
Troubled her song.

               I do not know if days
Or hours passed by, yet hold the morning rays
Shone many times among the glimmering flowers
Wove in her flower-like hair, before dark towers
Rose in the darkness, and the white surf gleamed
About them; and the horse of faery screamed
And shivered, knowing the Isle of many Fears,
Nor ceased until white Niam stroked his ears
And named him by sweet names.

                        A foaming tide
Whitened afar with surge, fan-formed and wide,
Burst from a great door marred by many a blow
From mace and sword and pole-axe, long ago
When gods and giants warred. We rode between
The seaweed-covered pillars, and the green
And surging phosphorus alone gave light
On our dark pathway, till a countless flight
Of moonlit steps glimmered; and left and right
Dark statues glimmered over the pale tide
Upon dark thrones. Between the lids of one
The imaged meteors had flashed and run
And had disported in the stilly jet,
And the fixed stars had dawned and shone and set,
Since God made Time and Death and Sleep: the other
Stretched his long arm to where, a misty smother,
The stream churned, churned, and churned—his lips apart,
As though he told his never slumbering heart
Of every foamdrop on its misty way:

Tying the horse to his vast foot that lay
Half in the unvesselled sea, we climbed the stairs
And climbed so long, I thought the last steps were
Hung from the morning star; when these mild words
Fanned the delighted air like wings of birds:
"My brothers spring out of their beds at morn,
A-murmur like young partridge: with loud horn
They chase the noontide deer;
And when the dew-drowned stars hang in the air
Look to long fishing-lines, or point and pare
A larch-wood hunting spear.

"O sigh, O fluttering sigh, be kind to me;
Flutter along the froth lips of the sea,
And shores, the froth lips wet:
And stay a little while, and bid them weep:
Ah, touch their blue veined eyelids if they sleep,
And shake their coverlet.

"When you have told how I weep endlessly,
Flutter along the froth lips of the sea
And home to me again,
And in the shadow of my hair lie hid,
And tell me how you came to one unbid,
The saddest of all men."

A maiden with soft eyes like funeral tapers,
And face that seemed wrought out of moonlit vapours,
And a sad mouth, that fear made tremulous
As any ruddy moth, looked down on us;
And she with a wave-rusted chain was tied
To two old eagles, full of ancient pride,
That with dim eyeballs stood on either side.
Few feathers were on their dishevelled wings,
For their dim minds were with the ancient things.

"I bring deliverance," pearl-pale Niam said.

"Neither the living, nor the unlabouring dead,
Nor the high gods who never lived, may fight
My enemy and hope; demons for fright
Jabber and scream about him in the night;

For he is strong and crafty as the seas
That sprang under the Seven Hazel Trees
And I must needs endure and hate and weep,
Until the gods and demons drop asleep
Hearing Aed touch the mournful strings of gold."

"Is he so dreadful?"
                              "Be not over bold,
But flee while you may flee from him."

                                        Then I:
"This demon shall be pierced and drop and die,
And his loose bulk be thrown in the loud tide."

"Flee from him," pearl-pale Niam weeping cried,
"For all men flee the demons;" but moved not,
Nor shook my firm and spacious soul one jot;
There was no mightier soul of Heber's line;
Now it is old and mouse-like: for a sign
I burst the chain: still earless, nerveless, blind,
Wrapped in the things of the unhuman mind,
In some dim memory or ancient mood
Still earless, nerveless, blind, the eagles stood.

And then we climbed the stair to a high door,
A hundred horsemen on the basalt floor
Beneath had paced content: we held our way
And stood within: clothed in a misty ray
I saw a foam-white seagull drift and float
Under the roof, and with a straining throat
Shouted, and hailed him: he hung there a star,
For no man's cry shall ever mount so far;
Not even your God could have thrown down that hall;
Stabling His unloosed lightnings in their stall,
He had sat down and sighed with cumbered heart,
As though His hour were come.

                                        We sought the par
That was most distant from the door; green slime
Made the way slippery, and time on time
Showed prints of sea-born scales, while down through it
The captives' journey to and fro were writ

Like a small river, and, where feet touched, came
A momentary gleam of phosphorus flame.
Under the deepest shadows of the hall
That maiden found a ring hung on the wall,
And in the ring a torch, and with its flare
Making a world about her in the air,
Passed under a dim doorway, out of sight,
And came again, holding a second light
Burning between her fingers, and in mine
Laid it and sighed: I held a sword whose shine
No centuries could dim: and a word ran
Thereon in Ogham letters, "Mananan":
That sea-god's name, who in a deep content
Sprang dripping, and, with captive demons sent
Out of the seven-fold seas, built the dark hall
Rooted in foam and clouds, and cried to all
The mightier masters of a mightier race;
And at his cry there came no milk-pale face
Under a crown of thorns and dark with blood,
But only exultant faces.

                    Niam stood
With bowed head, trembling when the white blade shone,
But she whose hours of tenderness were gone
Had neither hope nor fear. I bade them hide
Under the shadows till the tumults died
Of the loud crashing and earth shaking fight,
Lest they should look upon some dreadful sight;
And thrust the torch between the slimy flags.
A dome made out of endless carven jags,
Where shadowy face flowed into shadowy face,
Looked down on me; and in the self-same place
I waited hour by hour, and the high dome
Windowless, pillarless, multitudinous home
Of faces, waited; and the leisured gaze
Was loaded with the memory of days
Buried and mighty: when through the great door
The dawn came in, and glimmered on the floor
With a pale light, I journeyed round the hall
And found a door deep sunken in the wall,
The least of doors; beyond on a dim plain
A little runnel made a bubbling strain,

And on the runnel's stony and bare edge
A dusky demon dry as a withered sedge
Swayed, crooning to himself an unknown tongue:
In a sad revelry he sang and swung
Bacchant and mournful, passing to and fro
His hand along the runnel's side, as though
The flowers still grew there: far on the sea's waste;
Shaking and waving, vapour chased,
While high frail cloudlets, fed with a green light,
Like drifts of leaves, immovable and bright,
Hung in the passionate dawn. He slowly turned:
A demon's leisure: eyes, first white, now burned
Like wings of kingfishers; and he arose
Barking. We trampled up and down with blows
Of sword and brazen battle-axe, while day
Gave to high noon and noon to night gave way;
But when at withering of the sun he knew
The Druid sword of Mananan, he grew
To many shapes; I lunged at the smooth throat
Of a great eel; it changed, and I but smote
A fir-tree roaring in its leafless top;
I held a dripping corpse, with livid chop
And sunken shape, against my face and breast,
When I tore down the tree; but when the west
Surged up in plumy fire, I lunged and drave
Through heart and spine, and cast him in the wave,
Lest Niam shudder.

                    Full of hope and dread
Those two came carrying wine and meat and bread,
And healed my wounds with unguents out of flowers,
That feed white moths by some De Danaan shrine;
Then in that hall, lit by the dim sea shine,
We lay on skins of otters, and drank wine,
Brewed by the sea gods, from huge cups that lay
Upon the lips of sea-gods in their day;
And then on heaped-up skins of otters slept.
But when the sun once more in saffron stept,
Rolling his flagrant wheel out of the deep,
We sang the loves and angers without sleep,
And all the exultant labours of the strong:

But now the lying clerics murder song
With barren words and flatteries of the weak.
In what land do the powerless turn the beak
Of ravening Sorrow, or the hand of Wrath?
For all your croziers, they have left the path
And wander in the storms and clinging snows,
Hopeless for ever: ancient Oisin knows,
For he is weak and poor and blind, and lies
On the anvil of the world.

    S. PATRIC.   Be still: the skies
Are choked with thunder, lightning, and fierce wind,
For God has heard, and speaks His angry mind;
Go cast your body on the stones and pray,
For He has wrought midnight and dawn and day.

    OISIN. Saint, do you weep? I heard amid the thunder
The Fenian horses; armour torn asunder;
Laughter and cries: the armies clash and shock;
All is done now; I see the ravens flock;
Ah, cease, you mournful, laughing Fenian horn!

We feasted for three days. On the fourth morn
I found, dropping sea foam on the wide stair,
And hung with slime, and whispering in his hair,
That demon dull and unsubduable;
And once more to a day-long battle fell,
And at the sundown threw him in the surge,
To lie until the fourth morn saw emerge
His new healed shape: and for a hundred years
So warred, so feasted, with nor dreams, nor fears
Nor languor nor fatigue: an endless feast,
An endless war.

            The hundred years had ceased;
I stood upon the stair: the surges bore
A beech bough to me, and my heart grew sore,
Remembering how I stood by white-haired Finn
While the woodpecker made a merry din,
The hare leaped in the grass.

              Young Niam came
Holding that horse, and sadly called my name;
I mounted, and we passed over the lone

And drifting grayness, while this monotone,
Surly and distant, mixed inseparably
Into the clangour of the wind and sea.

"I hear my soul drop down into decay,
And Mananan's dark tower, stone by stone,
Gather sea slime and fall the seaward way,
And the moon goad the waters night and day,
That all be overthrown.

"But till the moon has taken all, I wage
War on the mightiest men under the skies,
And they have fallen or fled, age after age:
Light is man's love, and lighter is man's rage;
His purpose drifts and dies."

And then lost Niam murmured, "Love, we go
To the Island of Forgetfulness, for lo!
The Islands of Dancing and of Victories
Are empty of all power."

                    "And which of these
Is the Island of Content?"

                    "None know," she said;
And on my bosom laid her weeping head.

BOOK III

Fled foam underneath us, and round us, a wandering and
    milky smoke,
High as the saddle girth, covering away from our glances
    the tide;
And those that fled, and that followed, from the foam-pale
    distance broke;
The immortal desire of immortals we saw in their faces,
    and sighed.

I mused on the chase with the Fenians, and Bran, Sgeolan,
    Lomair,

And never a song sang Niam, and over my finger-tips
Came now the sliding of tears and sweeping of mist-cold
    hair,
And now the warmth of sighs, and after the quiver of lips.

Were we days long or hours long in riding, when rolled
    in a grisly peace,
An isle lay level before us, with dripping hazel and oak?
And we stood on a sea's edge we saw not; for whiter than
    new-washed fleece
Fled foam underneath us, and round us, a wandering and
    milky smoke.

And we rode on the plains of the sea's edge; the sea's edge
    barren and gray,
Gray sand on the green of the grasses and over the dripping
    trees,
Dripping and doubling landward, as though they would
    hasten away
Like an army of old men longing for rest from the moan
    of the seas.

But the trees grew taller and closer, immense in their
    wrinkling bark;
Dropping; a murmurous dropping; old silence and that
    one sound;
For no live creatures lived there, no weasels moved in the
    dark:
Long sighs arose in our spirits, beneath us bubbled the
    ground.

And the ears of the horse went sinking away in the hollow
    night,
For, as drift from a sailor slow drowning the gleams of the
    world and the sun,
Ceased on our hands and our faces, on hazel and oak leaf,
    the light,
And the stars were blotted above us, and the whole of the
    world was one.

Till the horse gave a whinny; for, cumbrous with stems
    of the hazel and oak,

A valley flowed down from his hoofs, and there in the long
    grass lay,
Under the starlight and shadow, a monstrous slumbering
    folk,
Their naked and gleaming bodies poured out and heaped
    in the way.

And by them were arrow and war-axe, arrow and shield
    and blade;
And dew-blanched horns, in whose hollow a child of three
    years old
Could sleep on a couch of rushes, and all inwrought and
    inlaid,
And more comely than man can make them with bronze
    and silver and gold.

And each of the huge white creatures was huger than
    fourscore men;
The tops of their ears were feathered, their hands were
    the claws of birds,
And, shaking the plumes of the grasses and the leaves of
    the mural glen,
The breathing came from those bodies, long-warless, grown
    whiter than curds.

The wood was so spacious above them, that He who had
    stars for His flocks
Could fondle the leaves with His fingers, nor go from His
    dew-cumbered skies;
So long were they sleeping, the owls had builded their nests
    in their locks,
Filling the fibrous dimness with long generations of eyes.

And over the limbs and the valley the slow owls wandered
    and came,
Now in a place of star-fire, and now in a shadow place
    wide,
And the chief of the huge white creatures, his knees in the
    soft star-flame,
Lay loose in a place of shadow: we drew the reins by his
    side.

Golden the nails of his bird-claws, flung loosely along the
     dim ground;
In one was a branch soft-shining, with bells more many
     than sighs,
In midst of an old man's bosom; owls ruffling and pacing
     around,
Sidled their bodies against him, filling the shade with their
     eyes.

And my gaze was thronged with the sleepers—no, neither
     in house of a cann
In a realm where the handsome are many, or in glamours
     by demons flung,
Are faces alive with such beauty made known to the salt
     eye of man,
Yet weary with passions that faded when the seven-fold
     seas were young.

And I gazed on the bell-branch, sleep's forbear, far sung
     by the Sennachies.
I saw how those slumberers, grown weary, there camping
     in grasses deep,
Of wars with the wide world and pacing the shores of the
     wandering seas,
Laid hands on the bell-branch and swayed it, and fed of
     unhuman sleep.

Snatching the horn of Niam, I blew a lingering note;
Came sound from those monstrous sleepers, a sound like
     the stirring of flies.
He, shaking the fold of his lips, and heaving the pillar of
     his throat,
Watched me with mournful wonder out of the wells of his
     eyes.

I cried, "Come out of the shadow, cann of the nails of
     gold!
And tell of your goodly household and the goodly works
     of your hands,
That we may muse in the starlight and talk of the battles
     of old;
Your questioner, Oisin, is worthy, he comes from the
     Fenian lands."

Half open his eyes were, and held me, dull with the smoke
    of their dreams;
His lips moved slowly in answer, no answer out of them
    came;
Then he swayed in his fingers the bell-branch, slow drop-
    ping a sound in faint streams
Softer than snow-flakes in April and piercing the marrow
    like flame.

Wrapt in the wave of the music, with weariness more than
    of earth,
The moil of my centuries filled me; and gone like a sea-
    covered stone
Were the memories of the whole of my sorrow and the
    memories of the whole of my mirth,
And a softness came from the starlight and filled me full
    to the bone.

In the roots of the grasses, the sorrels, I laid my body as
    low;
And the pearl-pale Niam lay by me, her brow on the midst
    of my breast;
And the horse was gone in the distance, and years after
    years 'gan flow;
Square leaves of the ivy moved over us, binding us down
    to our rest.

And, man of the many white croziers, a century there
    I forgot;
How the fetlocks drip blood in the battle, when the fallen
    on fallen lie rolled;
How the falconer follows the falcon in the weeds of the
    heron's plot,
And the names of the demons whose hammers made
    armour for Conhor of old

And, man of the many white croziers, a century there
    I forgot;
That the spear-shaft is made out of ashwood, the shield
    out of ozier and hide;
How the hammers spring on the anvil, on the spearhead's
    burning spot;

How the slow, blue-eyed oxen of Finn low sadly at evening
 tide.

But in dreams, mild man of the croziers, driving the dust
 with their throngs,
Moved round me, of seamen or landsmen, all who are
 winter tales;
Came by me the canns of the Red Branch, with roaring of
 laughter and songs,
Or moved as they moved once, love-making or piercing the
 tempest with sails.

Came Blanid, Mac Nessa, tall Fergus who feastward of old
 time slunk,
Cook Barach, the traitor; and warward, the spittle on his
 beard never dry,
Dark Balor, as old as a forest, car borne, his mighty head
 sunk
Helpless, men lifting the lids of his weary and death-
 making eye.

And by me, in soft red raiment, the Fenians moved in
 loud streams,
And Grania, walking and smiling, sewed with her needle
 of bone.
So lived I and lived not, so wrought I and wrought not,
 with creatures of dreams,
In a long iron sleep, as a fish in the water goes dumb as
 a stone.

At times our slumber was lightened. When the sun was on
 silver or gold;
When brushed with the wings of the owls, in the dimness
 they love going by;
When a glow-worm was green on a grass leaf, lured from
 his lair in the mould;
Half wakening, we lifted our eyelids, and gazed on the
 grass with a sigh.

So watched I when, man of the croziers, at the heel of a
 century fell,
Weak, in the midst of the meadow, from his miles in the
 midst of the air,

A starling like them that forgathered 'neath a moon waking
    white as a shell,
When the Fenians made foray at morning with Bran,
    Sgeolan, Lomair.

I awoke: the strange horse without summons out of the
    distance ran,
Thrusting his nose to my shoulder; he knew in his bosom
    deep
That once more moved in my bosom the ancient sadness
    of man,
And that I would leave the immortals, their dimness, their
    dews dropping sleep.

O, had you seen beautiful Niam grow white as the waters
    are white,
Lord of the croziers, you even had lifted your hands and
    wept:
But, the bird in my fingers, I mounted, remembering alone
    that delight
Of twilight and slumber were gone, and that hoofs im-
    patiently stept.

I cried, "O Niam! O white one! if only a twelve-houred
    day,
I must gaze on the beard of Finn, and move where the
    old men and young
In the Fenians' dwelling of wattle lean on the chessboards
    and play,
Ah, sweet to me now were even bald Conan's slanderous
    tongue!

"Like me were some galley forsaken far off in Meridian
    isle,
Remembering its long-oared companions, sails turning to
    thread-bare rags;
No more to crawl on the seas with long oars mile after mile,
But to be amid shooting of flies and flowering of rushes
    and flags."

Their motionless eyeballs of spirits grown mild with mys-
    terious thought,

Watched her those seamless faces from the valley's glim-
    mering girth;
As she murmured, "O wandering Oisin, the strength of the
    bell-branch is naught,
For there moves alive in your fingers the fluttering sadness
    of earth.

"Then go through the lands in the saddle and see what the
    mortals do,
And softly come to your Niam over the tops of the tide;
But weep for your Niam, O Oisin, weep; for if only your
    shoe
Brush lightly as haymouse earth's pebbles, you will come
    no more to my side.

"O flaming lion of the world, O when will you turn to your
    rest?"
I saw from a distant saddle; from the earth she made her
    moan;
"I would die like a small withered leaf in the autumn, for
    breast unto breast
We shall mingle no more, nor our gazes empty their sweet-
    ness lone

"In the isles of the farthest seas where only the spirits come
Were the winds less soft than the breath of a pigeon who
    sleeps on her nest,
Nor lost in the star-fires and odours the sound of the sea's
    vague drum
O flaming lion of the world, O when will you turn to your
    rest?"

The wailing grew distant; I rode by the woods of the
    wrinkling bark
Where ever is murmurous dropping, old silence and that
    one sound;
For no live creatures live there, no weasels move in the
    dark;
In a reverie forgetful of all things, over the bubbling ground.

And I rode by the plains of the sea's edge, where all is
    barren and gray,

Gray sands on the green of the grasses and over the
    dripping trees,
Dripping and doubling landward, as though they would
    hasten away,
Like an army of old men longing for rest from the moan
    of the seas.

And the winds made the sands on the sea's edge turning
    and turning go,
As my mind made the names of the Fenians. Far from
    the hazel and oak
I rode away on the surges, where, high as the saddle bow,
Fled foam underneath me, and round me, a wandering
    and milky smoke.

Long fled the foam-flakes around me, the winds fled out of
    the vast,
Snatching the bird in secret; nor knew I, embosomed apart,
When they froze the cloth on my body like armour riveted
    fast,
For Remembrance, lifting her leanness, keened in the gates
    of my heart.

Till fattening the winds of the morning, an odour of new-
    mown hay
Came, and my forehead fell low, and my tears like berries
    fell down;
Later a sound came, half lost in the sound of a shore far
    away,
From the great grass-barnacle calling, and later the shore-
    weeds brown.

If I were as I once was, the strong hoofs crushing the sand
    and the shells
Coming out of the sea as the dawn comes, a chaunt of
    love on my lips,
Not coughing, my head on my knees, and praying, and
    wroth with the bells,
I would leave no saint's head on his body from Rachlin
    to Bera of ships.

Making way from the kindling surges, I rode on a bridle-
    path

Much wondering to see upon all hands, of wattles and
    woodwork made,
Your bell-mounted churches, and guardless the sacred
    cairn and the rath,
And a small and feeble race stooping with mattock and
    spade.

Or weeding or ploughing with faces a-shining with much-
    toil wet;
While in this place and that place, with bodies unglorious,
    their chieftains stood,
Awaiting in patience the straw-death, croziered one, caught
    in your net:
Went the laughter of scorn from my mouth like the roaring
    of wind in a wood.

And because I went by them so huge and so speedy with
    eyes so bright,
Came after the hard gaze of youth, or an old man lifted
    his head:
And I rode and I rode, and I cried out, "The Fenians hunt
    wolves in the night,
So sleep they by daytime." A voice cried, "The Fenians
    a long time are dead."

A whitebeard stood hushed on the pathway, the flesh of
    his face as dried grass,
And in folds round his eyes and his mouth, he sad as a
    child without milk;
And the dreams of the islands were gone, and I knew how
    men sorrow and pass,
And their hound, and their horse, and their love, and their
    eyes that glimmer like silk.

And wrapping my face in my hair, I murmured, "In old
    age they ceased;"
And my tears were larger than berries, and I murmured,
    "Where white clouds lie spread
On Crevroe or broad Knockfefin, with many of old they
    feast
On the floors of the gods." He cried, "No, the gods a long
    time are dead."

And lonely and longing for Niam, I shivered and turned
    me about,
The heart in me longing to leap like a grasshopper into
    her heart;
I turned and rode to the westward, and followed the sea's
    old shout
Till I saw where Maive lies sleeping till starlight and mid-
    night part.

And there at the foot of the mountain, two carried a sack
    full of sand,
They bore it with staggering and sweating, but fell with
    their burden at length:
Leaning down from the gem-studded saddle, I flung it five
    yards with my hand,
With a sob for men waxing so weakly, a sob for the Fenians'
    old strength.

The rest you have heard of, O croziered one; how, when
    divided the girth,
I fell on the path, and the horse went away like a summer
    fly;
And my years three hundred fell on me, and I rose, and
    walked on the earth,
A creeping old man, full of sleep, with the spittle on his
    beard never dry.

How the men of the sand-sack showed me a church with
    its belfry in air;
Sorry place, where for swing of the war-axe in my dim eyes
    the crozier gleams;
What place have Caolte and Conan, and Bran, Sgeolan,
    Lomair?
Speak, you too are old with your memories, an old man
    surrounded with dreams.

S. PATRIC. When the flesh of the footsole clingeth on the
    burning stones is their place;
Where the demons whip them with wires on the burning
    stones of wide hell,
Watching the blessed ones move far off, and the smile on
    God's face,

Between them a gateway of brass, and the howl of the
    angels who fell.

OISIN. Put the staff in my hands; for I go to the Fenians,
    O cleric, to chaunt
The war-songs that roused them of old; they will rise, mak-
    ing clouds with their breath
Innumerable, singing, exultant; the clay underneath them
    shall pant,
And demons be broken in pieces, and trampled beneath
    them in death.

And demons afraid in their darkness; deep horror of eyes
    and of wings,
Afraid their ears on the earth laid, shall listen and rise up
    and weep;
Hearing the shaking of shields and the quiver of stretched
    bowstrings,
Hearing hell loud with a murmur, as shouting and mocking
    we sweep.

We will tear out the flaming stones, and batter the gateway
    of brass
And enter, and none sayeth "No" when there enters the
    strongly armed guest;
Make clean as a broom cleans, and march on as oxen move
    over young grass;
Then feast, making converse of Eire, of wars, and of old
    wounds, and rest.

S. PATRIC. On the flaming stones, without refuge, the
    limbs of the Fenians are tost;
None war on the masters of Hell, who could break up the
    world in their rage;
But kneel and wear out the flags and pray for your soul
    that is lost
Through the demon love of its youth and its godless and
    passionate age.

OISIN. Ah, me! to be shaken with coughing and broken
    with old age and pain,
Without laughter, a show unto children, alone with remem-
    brance and fear,

All emptied of purple hours as a beggar's cloak in the rain,
As a grass seed crushed by a pebble, as a wolf sucked
     under a weir.

It were sad to gaze on the blessed and no man I loved of
     old there;
I throw down the chain of small stones! when life in my
     body has ceased,
I will go to Caolte, and Conan, and Bran, Sgeolan, Lomair,
And dwell in the house of the Fenians, be they in flames
     or at feast.

TO THE ROSE UPON THE ROOD OF TIME

Red Rose, proud Rose, sad Rose of all my days!
Come near me, while I sing the ancient ways:
Cuchulain battling with the bitter tide;
The Druid, gray, wood-nurtured, quiet-eyed,
Who cast round Fergus dreams, and ruin untold;
And thine own sadness, whereof stars, grown old
In dancing silver sandalled on the sea,
Sing in their high and lonely melody.
Come near, that no more blinded by man's fate,
I find under the boughs of love and hate,
In all poor foolish things that live a day,
Eternal beauty wandering on her way.
Come near, come near, come near—Ah, leave me still
A little space for the rose-breath to fill!
Lest I no more hear common things that crave;
The weak worm hiding down in its small cave,
The field mouse running by me in the grass,
And heavy mortal hopes that toil and pass;
But seek alone to hear the strange things said
By God to the bright hearts of those long dead,
And learn to chaunt a tongue men do not know.
Come near; I would, before my time to go,

Sing of old Eire and the ancient ways:
Red Rose, proud Rose, sad Rose of all my days.

FERGUS AND THE DRUID

FERGUS. The whole day have I followed in the rocks,
And you have changed and flowed from shape to shape:
First as a raven on whose ancient wings
Scarcely a feather lingered; then you seemed
A weasel moving on from stone to stone;
And now at last you take on human shape—
A thin, grey man, half-lost in gathering night.

DRUID. What would you, king of the proud Red Branch
     kings?
FERGUS. This would I say, most wise of living souls:
Young, subtle Concobar sat close by me
When I gave judgment, and his words were wise,
And what to me was burden without end,
To him seemed easy; so I laid the crown
Upon his head to cast away my care.
DRUID. What would you, king of the proud Red Branch
     kings?
FERGUS. I feast amid my people on the hill,
And pace the woods, and drive my chariot wheels
In the white border of the murmuring sea,
But still I feel the crown upon my head.
DRUID. What would you?
FERGUS. I would be no more a king,
But learn the dreaming wisdom that is yours.
DRUID. Look on my thin grey hair and hollow cheeks,
And on these hands that may not lift the sword,
This body trembling like a wind-blown reed:
No maiden loves me, no man seeks my help,
Because I be not of the thing I dream.
FERGUS. A wild and foolish labourer is a king
To do and do and do, and never dream.

DRUID. Take then this small slate-coloured bag of
    dreams:
Unloose the cord, and they will wrap you round.
    FERGUS [having unloosed the cord]. I see my life go
        dripping like a stream
From change to change! I have been many things:
A green drop in the surge, a gleam of light
Upon a sword, a fir tree on a hill,
An old slave grinding at a heavy quern,
A king sitting upon a chair of gold;
And all these things were wonderful and great.
But now I have grown nothing, being all:
And in my heart the daemon and the gods
Wage an eternal battle, and I feel
The pain of wounds, the labour of the spear,
But have no share in loss or victory.

THE DEATH OF CUCHULAIN

A man came slowly from the setting sun,
To Forgail's daughter, Emer, in her dun,
And found her dyeing cloth with subtle care,
And said, casting aside his draggled hair:
"I am Aleel, the swineherd, whom you bid
Go dwell upon the sea cliffs, vapour hid;
But now my years of watching are no more."

Then Emer cast the web upon the floor,
And stretching out her arms, red with the dye,
Parted her lips with a loud sudden cry.

Looking on her, Aleel, the swineherd, said:
"Not any god alive, nor mortal dead,
Has slain so mighty armies, so great kings,
Nor won the gold that now Cuchulain brings."
"Why do you tremble thus from feet to crown?"

Aleel, the swineherd, wept and cast him down
Upon the web-heaped floor, and thus his word:
"With him is one sweet throated like a bird,
And lovelier than the moon upon the sea;
He made for her an army cease to be."

"Who bade you tell these things?" and then she cried
To those about, "Beat him with thongs of hide
And drive him from the door." And thus it was;
And where her son, Finmole, on the smooth grass
Was driving cattle, came she with swift feet,
And called out to him, "Son, it is not meet
That you stay idling here with flocks and herds."

"I have long waited, mother, for those words;
But wherefore now?"

                                    "There is a man to die;
You have the heaviest arm under the sky."
"My father dwells among the sea-worn bands,
And breaks the ridge of battle with his hands."

"Nay, you are taller than Cuchulain, son."
"He is the mightiest man in ship or dun."

"Nay, he is old and sad with many wars,
And weary of the crash of battle cars."

"I only ask what way my journey lies,
For God, who made you bitter, made you wise."

"The Red Branch kings a tireless banquet keep,
Where the sun falls into the Western deep.
Go there, and dwell on the green forest rim
But tell alone your name and house to him
Whose blade compels, and bid them send you one
Who has a like vow from their triple dun."
Between the lavish shelter of a wood
And the gray tide, the Red Branch multitude
Feasted, and with them old Cuchulain dwelt,
And his young dear one close beside him knelt,
And gazed upon the wisdom of his eyes,

More mournful than the depth of starry skies,
And pondered on the wonder of his days;
And all around the harpstring told his praise,
And Concobar, the Red Branch king of kings,
With his own fingers touched the brazen strings.
At last Cuchulain spake, "A young men strays
Driving the deer along the woody ways.
I often hear him singing to and fro
I often hear the sweet sound of his bow,
Seek out what man he is."

                              One went and came.
"He bade me let all know he gives his name
At the sword point, and bade me bring him one
Who had a like vow from our triple dun."

"I only of the Red Branch hosted now,"
Cuchulain cried, "have made and keep that vow."

After short fighting in the leafy shade,
He spake to the young man, "Is there no maid
Who loves you, no white arms to wrap you round,
Or do you long for the dim sleepy ground,
That you come here to meet this ancient sword?"
"The dooms of men are in God's hidden hoard."

"Your head a while seemed like a woman's head
That I loved once."

                              Again the fighting sped,
But now the war rage in Cuchulain woke,
And through the other's shield his long blade broke,
And pierced him.
                    "Speak before your breath is done."
"I am Finmole, mightly Cuchulain's son."
"I put you from your pain. I can no more."
While day its burden on to evening bore,
With head bowed on his knees Cuchulain stayed;
Then Concobar sent that sweet-throated maid,
And she, to win him, his gray hair caressed;
In vain her arms, in vain her soft white breast.
Then Concobar, the subtlest of all men,

Ranking his Druids round him ten by ten,
Spake thus, "Cuchulain will dwell there and brood,
For three days more in dreadful quietude,
And then arise, and raving slay us all.
Go, cast on him delusions magical,
That he might fight the waves of the loud sea."
And ten by ten under a quicken tree,
The Druids chaunted, swaying in their hands
Tall wands of alder and white quicken wands.

In three days' time, Cuchulain with a moan
Stood up, and came to the long sands alone:
For four days warred he with the bitter tide;
And the waves flowed above him, and he died.

ROSA MUNDI

Who dreamed that beauty passes like a dream?
For these red lips with all their mournful pride—
Mournful that no new wonder may betide—
Troy passed away in one high funeral gleam,
And Usna's children died.

We and the labouring world are passing by:
Amid men's souls that day by day give place,
More fleeting than the sea's foam-fickle face,
Under the passing stars, foam of the sky,
Lives on this lonely face.

Bow down, archangels, in your dim abode;
Before ye were, or any hearts to beat,
Weary and kind one stood beside His seat;
He made the worlds to be a grassy road
Before her wandering feet.

THE ROSE OF PEACE

If Michael, leader of God's host
When Heaven and Hell are met,
Looked down on you from Heaven's door-post
He would his deeds forget.

Brooding no more upon God's wars
In his Divine homestead,
He would go weave out of the stars
A chaplet for your head.

And all folk seeing him bow down,
And white stars tell your praise,
Would come at last to God's great town,
Led on by gentle ways;

And God would bid His warfare cease.
Saying all things were well;
And softly make a rosy peace,
A peace of Heaven with Hell.

THE ROSE OF BATTLE

Rose of all Roses, Rose of all the World!
The tall thought-woven sails, that flap unfurled
Above the tide of hours, trouble the air,
And God's bell buoyed to be the water's care;
While hushed from fear, or loud with hope, a band
With blown, spray-dabbled hair gather at hand.
Turn if you may from battles never done,
I call, as they go by me one by one,
Danger no refuge holds, and war no peace,
For him who hears love sing and never cease,
Beside her clean-swept hearth, her quiet shade:
But gather all for whom no love hath made

A woven silence, or but came to cast
A song into the air, and singing past
To smile on the pale dawn; and gather you
Who have sought more than is in rain or dew
Or in the sun and moon, or on the earth,
Or sighs amid the wandering, starry mirth,
Or comes in laughter from the sea's sad lips;
And wage God's battles in the long gray ships.
The sad, the lonely, the insatiable,
To these Old Night shall all her mystery tell;
God's bell has claimed them by the little cry
Of their sad hearts, that may not live nor die.

Rose of all Roses, Rose of all the World!
You, too, have come where the dim tides are hurled
Upon the wharves of sorrow, and heard ring
The bell that calls us on; the sweet far thing.
Beauty grown sad with its eternity
Made you of us, and of the dim gray sea.
Our long ships loose thought-woven sails and wait,
For God has bid them share an equal fate;
And when at last defeated in His wars,
They have gone down under the same white stars,
We shall no longer hear the little cry
Of our sad hearts, that may not live nor die.

A FAIRY SONG

Sung by "the Good People" over the outlaw
Michael Dwyer and his bride, who had escaped
into the mountains.

We who are old, old and gay,
O so old,
Thousands of years, thousands of years,
If all were told:

Give to these children new from the world,
Silence and love,
And the long dew-dropping hours of the night
And the stars above:

Give to these children new from the world,
Rest far from men.
Is anything better, anything better?
Tell it us then:

Us who are old, old and gay,
O so old,
Thousands of years, thousands of years,
If all were told.

THE LAKE ISLE OF INNISFREE

I will arise and go now, and go to Innisfree,
And a small cabin build there, of clay and wattles made;
Nine bean rows will I have there, a hive for the honey bee,
And live alone in the bee-loud glade.

And I shall have some peace there, for peace comes
        dropping slow,
Dropping from the veils of the morning to where
        the cricket sings;
There midnight's all a glimmer, and noon a purple glow,
And evening full of the linnet's wings.

I will arise and go now, for always night and day
I hear lake water lapping with low sounds by the shore;
While I stand on the roadway, or on the pavements gray,
I hear it in the deep heart's core.

THE PITY OF LOVE

A pity beyond all telling
Is hid in the heart of love:
The folk who are buying and selling;
The clouds on their journey above;
The cold wet winds ever blowing;
And the shadowy hazel grove
Where mouse-gray waters are flowing
Threaten the head that I love.

THE SORROW OF LOVE

The quarrel of the sparrows in the eaves,
The full round moon and the star-laden sky,
And the loud song of the ever-singing leaves,
Had hid away earth's old and weary cry.

And then you came with those red mournful lips,
And with you came the whole of the world's tears,
And all the trouble of her labouring ships,
And all the trouble of her myriad years.

And now the sparrows warring in the eaves,
The curd-pale moon, the white stars in the sky,
And the loud chaunting of the unquiet leaves,
Are shaken with earth's old and weary cry.

WHEN YOU ARE OLD

When you are old and gray and full of sleep,
And nodding by the fire, take down this book,

And slowly read, and dream of the soft look
Your eyes had once, and of their shadows deep;

How many loved your moments of glad grace,
And loved your beauty with love false or true
But one man loved the pilgrim soul in you,
And loved the sorrows of your changing face.

And bending down beside the glowing bars
Murmur, a little sadly, how love fled
And paced upon the mountains overhead
And hid his face amid a crowd of stars.

THE WHITE BIRDS

I would that we were, my beloved, white birds on the
        foam of the sea!
We tire of the flame of the meteor, before it can
        fade and flee;
And the flame of the blue star of twilight, hung low on
        the rim of the sky,
Has awaked in our hearts, my beloved, a sadness
        that may not die.

A weariness comes from those dreamers, dew dabbled, the
        lily and rose;
Ah, dream not of them, my beloved, the flame of the
        meteor that goes,
Or the flame of the blue star that lingers hung low in
        the fall of the dew:
For I would we were changed to white birds on the
        wandering foam: I and you!

I am haunted by numberless islands, and many
        a Danaan shore,
Where Time would surely forget us, and Sorrow come
        near us no more;
Soon far from the rose and the lily, and fret of the
        flames would we be,

Were we only white birds, my beloved, buoyed out on
    the foam of the sea!

A DREAM OF DEATH

I dreamed that one had died in a strange place
Near no accustomed hand;
And they had nailed the boards above her face,
The peasants of that land,
And, wondering, planted by her solitude
A cypress and a yew:
I came, and wrote upon a cross of wood,
Man had no more to do:
She was more beautiful than thy first love,
This lady by the trees:
And gazed upon the mournful stars above,
And heard the mournful breeze.

THE MAN WHO DREAMED OF
FAERYLAND

He stood among a crowd at Drumahair;
His heart hung all upon a silken dress,
And he had known at last some tenderness,
Before earth made of him her sleepy care;
But when a man poured fish into a pile,
It seemed they raised their little silver heads,
And sang how day a Druid twilight sheds
Upon a dim, green, well-beloved isle,
Where people love beside star-laden seas;
How Time may never mar their faery vows
Under the woven roofs of quicken boughs:
The singing shook him out of his new ease.

He wandered by the sands of Lisadill;
His mind ran all on money cares and fears,

And he had known at last some prudent years
Before they heaped his grave under the hill;
But while he passed before a plashy place,
A lug-worm with its gray and muddy mouth
Sang how somewhere to north or west or south
There dwelt a gay, exulting, gentle race;
And how beneath those three times blessed skies
A Danaan fruitage makes a shower of moons,
And as it falls awakens leafy tunes:
And at that singing he was no more wise.

He mused beside the well of Scanavin,
He mused upon his mockers: without fail
His sudden vengeance were a country tale,
Now that deep earth has drunk his body in;
But one small knot-grass growing by the pool
Told where, ah, little, all-unneeded voice!
Old Silence bids a lonely folk rejoice,
And chaplet their calm brows with leafage cool;
And how, when fades the sea-strewn rose of day,
A gentle feeling wraps them like a fleece,
And all their trouble dies into its peace:
The tale drove his fine angry mood away.

He slept under the hill of Lugnagall;
And might have known at last unhaunted sleep
Under that cold and vapour-turbaned steep,
Now that old earth had taken man and all:
Were not the worms that spired about his bones
A-telling with their low and reedy cry,
Of how God leans His hands out of the sky,
To bless that isle with honey in His tones;
That none may feel the power of squall and wave,
And no one any leaf-crowned dancer miss
Until He burn up Nature with a kiss:
The man has found no comfort in the grave.

THE LAMENTATION OF THE OLD PENSIONER

I had a chair at every hearth,
When no one turned to see,
With "Look at that old fellow there,
And who may he be?"
And therefore do I wander now,
And the fret lies on me.

The road-side trees keep murmuring
Ah, wherefore murmur ye,
As in the old days long gone by,
Green oak and poplar tree?
The well-known faces are all gone
And the fret lies on me.

THE BALLAD OF FATHER GILLIGAN

The old priest Peter Gilligan
Was weary night and day;
For half his flock were in their beds,
Or under green sods lay.

Once, while he nodded on a chair,
At the moth-hour of eve,
Another poor man sent for him,
And he began to grieve.

"I have no rest, nor joy, nor peace,
For people die and die";
And after cried he, "God forgive!
My body spake, not I!"

He knelt, and leaning on the chair
He prayed and fell asleep;

And the moth-hour went from the fields,
And stars began to peep.

They slowly into millions grew,
And leaves shook in the wind;
And God covered the world with shade,
And whispered to mankind.

Upon the time of sparrow chirp
When the moths came once more,
The old priest Peter Gilligan
Stood upright on the floor.

"Mavrone, mavrone! the man has died,
While I slept on the chair";
He roused his horse out of its sleep,
And rode with little care.

He rode now as he never rode,
By rocky lane and fen;
The sick man's wife opened the door:
"Father! you come again!"

"And is the poor man dead?" he cried.
"He died an hour ago,"
The old priest Peter Gilligan
In grief swayed to and fro.

"When you were gone, he turned and died
As merry as a bird."
The old priest Peter Gilligan
He knelt him at that word.

"He who hath made the night of stars
For souls, who tire and bleed,
Sent one of His great angels down
To help me in my need.

"He who is wrapped in purple robes,
With planets in His care,
Had pity on the least of things
Asleep upon a chair."

THE TWO TREES

Beloved, gaze in thine own heart,
The holy tree is growing there;
From joy the holy branches start,
And all the trembling flowers they bear.
The changing colours of its fruit
Have dowered the stars with merry light;
The surety of its hidden root
Has planted quiet in the night;
The shaking of its leafy head
Has given the waves their melody,
And made my lips and music wed,
Murmuring a wizard song for thee.
There, through bewildered branches, go
Winged Loves borne on in gentle strife,
Tossing and tossing to and fro
The flaming circle of our life.
When looking on their shaken hair,
And dreaming how they dance and dart,
Thine eyes grow full of tender care:
Beloved, gaze in thine own heart.

Gaze no more in the bitter glass
The demons, with their subtle guile,
Lift up before us when they pass,
Or only gaze a little while;
For there a fatal image grows,
With broken boughs, and blackened leaves,
And roots half hidden under snows
Driven by a storm that ever grieves.
For all things turn to barrenness
In the dim glass the demons hold,
The glass of outer weariness,
Made when God slept in times of old.
There, through the broken branches, go
The ravens of unresting thought;
Peering and flying to and fro,
To see men's souls bartered and bought.
When they are heard upon the wind,

And when they shake their wings; alas!
Thy tender eyes grow all unkind:
Gaze no more in the bitter glass.

TO IRELAND IN THE COMING TIMES

Know, that I would accounted be
True brother of that company,
Who sang to sweeten Ireland's wrong,
Ballad and story, rann and song;
Nor be I any less of them,
Because the red-rose-bordered hem
Of her, whose history began
Before God made the angelic clan,
Trails all about the written page;
For in the world's first blossoming age
The light fall of her flying feet
Made Ireland's heart begin to beat;
And still the starry candles flare
To help her light foot here and there;
And still the thoughts of Ireland brood
Upon her holy quietude.

Nor may I less be counted one
With Davis, Mangan, Ferguson,
Because to him, who ponders well,
My rhymes more than their rhyming tell
Of the dim wisdoms old and deep,
That God gives unto man in sleep.
For the elemental beings go
About my table to and fro.
In flood and fire and clay and wind,
They huddle from man's pondering mind;
Yet he who treads in austere ways
May surely meet their ancient gaze.
Man ever journeys on with them

After the red-rose-bordered hem.
Ah, faeries, dancing under the moon,
A Druid land, a Druid tune!

While still I may, I write for you
The love I lived, the dream I knew.
From our birthday, until we die,
Is but the winking of an eye;
And we, our singing and our love,
The mariners of night above,
And all the wizard things that go
About my table to and fro,
Are passing on to where may be,
In truth's consuming ecstasy,
No place for love and dream at all;
For God goes by with white foot-fall.
I cast my heart into my rhymes,
That you, in the dim coming times,
May know how my heart went with them
After the red-rose-bordered hem.

THE EVERLASTING VOICES

O sweet everlasting voices be still;
Go to the guards of the heavenly fold
And bid them wander obeying your will
Flame under flame, till Time be no more;
Have you not heard that our hearts are old,
That you call in birds, in wind on the hill,
In shaken boughs, in tide on the shore?
O sweet everlasting Voices be still.

THE MOODS

Time drops in decay,
Like a candle burnt out,
And the mountains and woods
Have their day, have their day;
What one in the rout
Of the fire-born moods,
Has fallen away?

THE STOLEN BRIDE

O'Driscoll drove with a song
The wild duck and the drake
From the tall and the tufted reeds
Of the dear Heart Lake.

And he saw how the reeds grew dark
At the coming of night-tide,
And dreamed of the long dim hair
Of Bridget his bride.

He heard while he sang and dreamed
A piper piping away,
And never was piping so sad,
And never was piping so gay.

And he saw young men and young girls
Who danced on a level place,
And Bridget his bride among them,
With a sad and a gay face.

The dancers crowded about him
And many a sweet thing said,
And a young man brought him red wine,
And a young girl white bread.

But Bridget drew him by the sleeve
Away from the merry bands,
To old men playing cards,
With a twinkling of ancient hands.

The bread and the wine had a doom,
For these were the folk of the air;
He sat down and played in a dream
Of her long dim hair.

He played with the merry old men,
And thought not of evil chance,
Until one bore Bridget his bride
Away from the merry dance.

He bore her away in his arms,
The handsomest young man there,
And his neck and his breast and his arms
Were drowned in her long dim hair.

O'Driscoll got up from the grass,
And scattered the cards with a cry,
But the old men and dancers were gone,
As a cloud faded into the sky.

He knew now the folk of the air,
And his heart was blackened by dread,
And he ran to the door of his house;
Old women were keening the dead;

But he heard high up in the air
A piper piping away;
And never was piping so sad,
And never was piping so gay.

THE SONG OF WANDERING AENGUS

I went out to the hazel wood,
Because a fire was in my head,
And cut and peeled a hazel wand,
And hooked a berry to a thread;
And when white moths were on the wing,
And moth-like stars were flickering out,
I dropped the berry in a stream
And caught a little silver trout.

When I had laid it on the floor
I went to blow the fire a-flame,
But something rustled on the floor,
And some one called me by my name:

It had become a glimmering girl
With apple blossom in her hair
Who called me by my name and ran
And faded through the brightening air.

Though I am old with wandering
Through hollow lands and hilly lands,
I will find out where she has gone,
And kiss her lips and take her hands;
And walk among long dappled grass,
And pluck till time and times are done,
The silver apples of the moon,
The golden apples of the sun.

THE FIDDLER OF DOONEY

When I play on my fiddle in Dooney,
Folk dance like a wave of the sea;
My cousin is priest in Kilvarnet,
My brother in Moharabuiee.

I passed my brother and cousin:
They read in their books of prayers;
I read in my book of songs
I bought at the Sligo fair.

When we come at the end of time,
To Peter sitting in state,
He will smile on the three old spirits,
But call me first through the gate;

For the good are always the merry,
Save by an evil chance,
And the merry love the fiddle
And the merry love to dance:

And when the folk there spy me,
They will all come up to me,
With "Here is the fiddler of Dooney!"
And dance like a wave of the sea.

MONGAN LAMENTS THE CHANGE THAT HAS COME UPON HIM AND HIS BELOVED

Do you not hear me calling, white deer with no horns!
I have been changed to a hound with one red ear;
I have been in the Path of Stones and the Wood of Thorns,
For somebody hid hatred and hope and desire and fear
Under my feet that they follow you night and day.
A man with a hazel wand came without sound;
He changed me suddenly; I was looking another way;
And now my calling is but the calling of a hound;
And Time and Birth and Change are hurrying by.
I would that the boar without bristles had come from the
    West
And had rooted the sun and moon and stars out of the sky
And lay in the darkness, grunting, and turning to his rest.

O'SULLIVAN RUA TO MARY LAVELL

When my arms wrap you round, I press
My heart upon the loveliness
That has long faded in the world;
The jewelled crowns that kings have hurled
In shadowy pools, when armies fled;
The love-tales wove with silken thread
By dreaming ladies upon cloth
That has made fat the murderous moth;
The roses that of old time were
Woven by ladies in their hair,
Before they drowned their lovers' eyes
In twilight shaken with low sighs;
The dew-cold lilies ladies bore
Through many a sacred corridor
Where a so sleepy incense rose
That only God's eyes did not close:
For that dim brow and lingering hand
Come from a more dream-heavy land,
A more dream-heavy hour than this;
And, when you sigh from kiss to kiss,
I hear pale Beauty sighing too,
For hours when all must fade like dew
Till there be naught but throne on throne
Of seraphs, brooding, each alone,
A sword upon his iron knees
On her most lonely mysteries.

AEDH GIVES HIS BELOVED CERTAIN RHYMES

"Fasten your hair with a golden pin,
And bind up every wandering tress;
I bade my heart build these poor rhymes:

It worked at them day out, day in,
Building a sorrowful loveliness
Out of the battles of old times.

"You need but lift a pearl-pale hand,
And bind up your long hair and sigh;
And all men's hearts must burn and beat;
And candle-like foam on the dim sand,
And stars climbing the dew-dropping sky,
Live but to light your passing feet."

CAP AND BELL

A Queen was loved by a jester,
And once, when the owls grew still,
He made his soul go upward
And stand on her window sill.

In a long and straight blue garment
It talked, ere the morn grew white.
It had grown most wise with thinking
On a foot-fall hushed and light,

But the young Queen would not listen:
She rose in her pale night-gown,
She drew in the brightening casement,
She snicked the brass bolts down.

He bade his heart go to her,
When the bats cried out no more:
In a garment red and quivering,
It sang to her through the door,

The tongue of it sweet with dreaming
On a flutter of flower-like hair;
But she took her fan from the table,
And waved it out on the air.

"I've cap and bells" (he pondered),
"I will send them to her and die."
And as soon as the morn had whitened,
He left them where she went by.

She took them into her bosom,
In her heart she found a tune,
Her red lips sang them a love-song,
The night smelled rich with June.

She opened the door and her window,
The heart and the soul came through:
To her right hand came the red one,
To her left hand came the blue.

They set up a noise like crickets,
And a chattering wise and sweet;
And her hair was a folded flower,
And the quiet of love in her feet.

THE VALLEY OF THE BLACK PIG

The dews drop slowly and dreams gather: unknown spears
Suddenly hurtle before my dream-awakened eyes,
And then the clash of fallen horsemen and the cries
Of unknown perishing armies beat about my ears.
We who still labour by the cromlec on the shore,
The grey cairn on the hill, when day sinks drowned in dew,
Being weary of the world's empires, bow down to you
Master of the still stars and of the flaming door.

THE TWILIGHT OF FORGIVENESS

If this importunate heart trouble your peace
With words lighter than air,
And hopes that in mere hoping flicker and cease:
Crush the rose in your hair,
Cover your lips with rose-heavy twilight, and say:
"O hearts of wind-blown flame!
O winds, elder than changing of night and day,
That longing and murmuring came
From marble cities loud with tabors of old
In dove-gray faery lands,
From battle-banners fold upon purple fold
Queens wrought with glimmering hands;
That saw young Niam hover with love-lorn face
Above the wandering tide;
And lingered in the hidden desolate place
Where the last phoenix died
And gathered the flames above his holy head,
And still murmur and long:
O piteous hearts, changing till change be dead
In a tumultuous song."
Then cover the pale blossom of your breast
With your dim shadowy hair,
And trouble with sighs for all hearts without rest
The rose-heavy twilight there.

THE VALLEY OF LOVERS

I dreamed that I stood in a valley, and amid sighs,
For happy lovers passed, two by two, where I stood;
And I dreamed my lost love came stealthily out of the wood
With her cloud-pale eyelids half covering her dim eyes:
And I cried in my dream "O women, bid the young men lay
Their heads on your knees, and drown their eyes with your
    hair,

Or, remembering hers, they will hold no other face fair
Till the valleys of the world have been withered away."

POEM BY O'SULLIVAN THE RED
CONCERNING MARY LAVELL I

O daughter of the Island of Woods;
We poets labour all our days,
To build the perfect beauty in rhyme,
Still overthrown by a woman's gaze,
And by the heaven's unlabouring broods;
And therefore my heart bows down anew,
At hush of evening till God burn Time
Before unlabouring stars and you.

THE SECRET ROSE

Far off, most secret, and inviolate Rose,
Enfold me in my hour of hours; where those
Who sought thee in the Holy Sepulchre,
Or in the wine vat, dwell beyond the stir
And tumult of defeated dreams; and deep
Among pale eyelids, heavy with the sleep
Men have named beauty. Thy great leaves enfold
The ancient beards, the helms of ruby and gold
Of the crowned Magi; and the king whose eyes
Saw the Pierced Hands and Rood of elder rise
In druid vapour and make the torches dim;
Till vain frenzy awoke and he died; and him
Who met Fand walking among flaming dew
By a gray shore where the wind never blew,
And lost the world and Emer for a kiss;

And him who drove the gods out of their liss,
And till a hundred morns had flowered red,
Feasted and wept the barrows of his dead;
And the proud dreaming king who flung the crown
And sorrow away, and calling bard and clown
Dwelt among wine-stained wanderers in deep woods;
And him who sold tillage, and house, and goods,
And sought through lands and islands numberless
      years,
Until he found with laughter and with tears,
A woman of so shining loveliness,
That men threshed corn at midnight by a tress,
A little stolen tress. I, too, await
The hour of thy great wind of love and hate.
When shall the stars be blown about the sky,
Like the sparks blown out of a smithy, and die?
Surely thine hour has come, thy great wind blows,
Far off, most secret, and inviolate Rose?

O'SULLIVAN THE RED UPON HIS WANDERINGS

O where is our Mother of Peace
Nodding her purple hood?
The winds that awakened the stars
Are blowing through my blood.
I would the pale deer had come
From Gulleon's place of pride,
And trampled the mountains away,
And drunk up the murmuring tide;
For the winds that awakened the stars
Are blowing through my blood,
And our Mother of Peace has forgot me
Under her purple hood.

THE TRAVAIL OF PASSION

When the flaming, lute-thronged angelic door is wide;
When an immortal passion breathes in mortal clay,
Our hearts endure the plaited thorn, the crowded way
The knotted scourge, the nail-pierced hands, the
        wounded side,
The hissop-heavy sponge, the flowers by Kidron stream:
We will bend down, and loosen our hair over you
That it may drop faint perfume and be heavy with dew,
Lilies of death-pale hope, roses of passionate dream.

HANRAHAN SPEAKS TO THE LOVERS OF HIS SONGS IN COMING DAYS

O, Colleens, kneeling by your altar rails long hence,
When songs I wove for my beloved hide the prayer,
And smoke from this dead heart drifts through the violet
        air
And covers away the smoke of myrrh and frankincense;
Bend down and pray for the great sin I wove in song,
Till Maurya of the wounded heart cry a sweet cry,
And call to my beloved and me: "No longer fly
Amid the hovering, piteous, penitential throng."

AEDH WISHES HIS BELOVED WERE DEAD

Were you but lying cold and dead,
And lights were paling out of the West,

You would come hither, and bend your head,
And I would lay my head on your breast;
And you would murmur tender words,
Forgiving me, because you were dead:
Nor would you rise and hasten away,
Though you have the will of the wild birds,
But know your hair was bound and wound
About the stars and moon and sun:
O would beloved that you lay
Under the dock-leaves in the ground,
While lights were paling one by one.

AEDH WISHES FOR THE CLOTHS
OF HEAVEN

Had I the heavens' embroidered cloths,
Enwrought with golden and silver light,
The blue and the dim and the dark cloths
Of night and light and the half light,
I would spread the cloths under your feet:
But I, being poor, have only my dreams;
I have spread my dreams under your feet;
Tread softly because you tread on my dreams.

IN THE SEVEN WOODS

I have heard the pigeons of the Seven Woods
Make their faint thunder, and the garden bees
Hum in the lime tree flowers; and put away
The unavailing outcries and the old bitterness
That empty the heart. I have forgot awhile
Tara uprooted, and new commonness

Upon the throne and crying about the streets
And hanging its paper flowers from post to post,
Because it is alone of all things happy.
I am contented for I know that Quiet
Wanders laughing and eating her wild heart
Among pigeons and bees, while that Great Archer,
Who but awaits His hour to shoot, still hangs
A cloudy quiver over Parc-na-Lee.
  August, 1902.

THE ARROW

I thought of your beauty and this arrow
Made out of a wild thought is in my marrow.
There's no man may look upon her, no man,
As when newly grown to be a woman,
Blossom pale, she pulled down the pale blossom
At the moth hour and hid it in her bosom.
This beauty's kinder yet for a reason
I could weep that the old is out of season.

OLD MEMORY

O thought fly to her when the end of day
Awakens an old memory, and say
"Your strength, that is so lofty and fierce and kind
It might call up a new age, calling to mind
The queens that were imagined long ago,
Is but half yours; he kneaded in the dough
Through the long days of youth, and who would have
    thought
It all and more than it all would come to naught

And that dear words meant nothing?"—but enough,
For when we have blamed the wind we can blame love,
Or, if there needs be more, be nothing said
That had been harsh for children that have strayed.

UNTITLED SONG

The old brown thorn trees break in two high over
    Cumann's strand,
Under a bitter black wind that blows from the left hand.
Our courage breaks like an old tree in a black wind and
    dies,
But we have hidden in our hearts the flame out of the eyes
Of Cathleen, the daughter of Houlihan.

The wind has bundled up the clouds high over Knocknarea,
And thrown the thunder on the stones for all that Maeva
    can say;
Angers that are like noisy clouds have set our hearts
    abeat,
But we have all bent low and low and kissed the quiet feet
Of Cathleen, the daughter of Houlihan.

The yellow pool has overflowed high up on Clooth-na-
    Bare,
For the wet winds are blowing out of the clinging air;
Like heavy flooded waters are our bodies and our blood,
But purer than a tall candle before the Holy Rood
Is Cathleen, the daughter of Houlihan.

THE PLAYERS ASK FOR A BLESSING ON THE PSALTERIES AND THEMSELVES

THREE VOICES TOGETHER. Hurry to bless the hands that play
The mouths that speak, the notes and strings
O masters of the glittering town!
O! lay the shrilly trumpet down,
Though drunken with the flags that sway
Over the ramparts and the towers,
And with the waving of your wings.
  FIRST VOICE. Maybe they linger by the way;
One gathers up his purple gown;
One leans and mutters by the wall;
He dreads the weight of mortal hours.
  SECOND VOICE. O no, O no; they hurry down
Like plovers that have heard the call.
  THIRD VOICE. O, kinsmen of the Three in One,
O, kinsmen bless the hands that play.
The notes they waken shall live on
When all this heavy history's done.
Our hands, our hands must ebb away.
  THREE VOICES TOGETHER. The proud and careless notes
    live on
But bless our hands that ebb away.

THE OLD AGE OF QUEEN MAEVE

Maeve, the great queen, was pacing to and fro,
Between the walls covered with beaten bronze
In her high house at Cruachan; the long hearth,
Flickering with ash and hazel, but half showed
Where the tired horse-boys lay upon the rushes,
Or on the benches underneath the walls,

In comfortable sleep. All living slept;
But that great queen, who more than half the night
Had paced from door to fire, and fire to door.
Though now in her old age, in her young age
She had been beautiful in that old way
That's all but gone, for the proud heart is gone,
And the fool heart of the counting-house fears all
But soft beauty and indolent desire.
She could have called over the rim of the world
Whatever woman's lover had hit her fancy,
And yet had been great bodied and great limbed,
Fashioned to be the mother of strong children,
And she'd had lucky eyes and a high heart,
And wisdom that caught fire like the dried flax,
At need, and made her beautiful and fierce,
Sudden and laughing.
                                    O, unquiet heart,
Why do you praise another, praising her
As if there were no tale but your own tale
Worth knitting to a measure of sweet sound,
Have I not bid you tell of that great queen
Who has been buried some two thousand years?

When night was at its deepest, a wild goose
Cried from the porter's lodge, and with long clamour
Shook the ale-horns and shields upon their hooks,
But the horse-boys slept on, as though some power
Had filled the house with Druid heaviness;
And wondering who of the many-changing Sidhe
Had come, as in old times, to counsel her,
Maeve walked, yet with slow footfall, being old,
To that small chamber by the outer gate.

The porter slept, although he sat upright
With still and stony limbs and open eyes.
Maeve waited, and when that ear-piercing noise
Broke from his parted lips, and broke again,
She laid a hand on either of his shoulders
And shook him wide awake, and bid him say
Who of the wandering many-changing ones
Had troubled his sleep. But all he had to say
Was that the air, being heavy, and the dogs

More still than they had been for a good month,
He had fallen asleep, and though he had dreamed nothing,
He could remember when he had had fine dreams,
It was before the time of the great war
Over the White-horned Bull, and the Brown Bull.

She turned away; he turned again to sleep,
That no god troubled now, and, wondering
What matters were afoot among the Sidhe,
Maeve walked through that great hall, and with a sigh
Lifted the curtain of her sleeping-room,
Remembering that she too had seemed divine
To many thousand eyes, and to her own
One that the generations had long waited
That work too difficult for mortal hands
Might be accomplished. Bunching the curtain up
She saw her husband, Ailell, sleeping there,
And thought of days when he'd had a straight body,
And of that famous Fergus, Nessa's husband,
Who had been the lover of her middle life.

Suddenly Ailell spoke out of his sleep,
And not with his own voice, or a man's voice,
But with the burning, live, unshaken voice
Of those that it may be shall never fade.
He said, "High queen of Cruachan and Magh Ai,
A king of the Great Plain would speak with you."
And with glad voice Maeve answered him, "What king
Of the far wandering shadows has come to me,
As in the old days, when they would come and go
About my threshold to counsel and to help?"
The parted lips replied, "I seek your help,
For I am Aengus, and I am crossed in love."

"How may a mortal whose life gutters out,
Help them that wander, with hand clasping hand,
By rivers where the rain has never dimmed
Their haughty images that cannot fade
For all their beauty, like a hollow dream?"
"I come from the undimmed rivers to bid you call
The children of the Maines out of sleep,
And set them digging into Anbual's hill.

We shadows, while they uproot his earthy house,
Will overthrow his shadows, and carry off
Caer, his blue-eyed daughter, that I love.
I helped your fathers when they built these walls,
And I would have your help in my great need,
Queen of high Cruachan."

                "I obey your will
With speedy feet and a most thankful heart,
For you have been, O Aengus of the birds,
Our giver of good counsel and good luck."
And with a groan as if the mortal breath
Could but awaken sadly upon lips
That happier breath had moved, her husband turned
Face downward, tossing in a troubled sleep;
But Maeve, and not with a slow, feeble foot,
Came to the threshold of the painted house,
Where her grand-children slept, and cried aloud
Until the pillared dark began to stir
With shouting and the clang of unhooked arms.

She told them of the many-changing ones;
And all that night, and all through the next day
To middle night they dug into the hill.
At middle night, great cats with silver claws,
Bodies of shadow, and blind eyes like pearls,
Came up out of the hole, and red-eared hounds
With long white bodies came out of the air
Suddenly, and ran at them and harried them.

The Maines' children dropped their spades and stood
With quaking joints and terror-stricken faces,
Till Maeve called out, "These are but common men,
The Maines' children have not dropped their spades
Because Earth, crazy for its broken power,
Casts up a show, and the winds answer it
With holy shadows." Her high heart was glad,
And when the uproar ran along the grass,
She followed with light footfall in the midst,
Till it died out where an old thorn tree stood.
Friend of these many years, you to have stood

With equal courage in that whirling rout,
For you, although you have not her wandering heart,
Have all that greatness, and not hers alone,
For there is no high story about queens
In any ancient book but tells of you,
And when I've heard how they grew old and died,
Or fell into unhappiness, I've said,
"She will grow old, and die, and she has wept,"
And when I'd write it out anew, the words
Half crazy with the thought, "she too has wept,"
Outrun the measure.
                          I'd tell of that great queen,
Who stood amid a silence by the thorn
Until two lovers came out of the air
With bodies made out of soft fire. The one
About whose face birds wagged their fiery wings
Said, "Aengus and his sweetheart give their thanks
To Maeve and to Maeve's household, owing all
In owing them the bride-bed that gives peace."
Then Maeve, "O, Aengus, master of all lovers,
A thousand years ago you held high talk
With the first kings of many-pillared Cruachan,
O, when will you grow weary?"
                          They had vanished,
But out of the dark air over her head there came
A murmur of soft words and meeting lips.

NOTES ON THE POEMS

Note on the text of *The Celtic Twilight*: The text is a reprint of the edition published by A. H. Bullen and Company, London, in 1902. The quotation marks have been changed to conform with modern American usage.

"Miserrimus." Retitled "The Sad Shepherd" in *Poems*, 1895.

"Voices." Retitled "The Cloak, the Boat, and the Shoes" in *Poems*, 1895. This poem and "Miserrimus" were part of an Arcadian play, *The Island of Statues*. It is a romantic work showing the influence of Spenser and Shelley.

"The Indian to His Love." This poem and "The Indian upon God" were written in 1886 under the spell of the Brahmin, Mohini Chatterjee, whom Yeats and his friends had invited to Dublin.

"Down by the Salley Gardens." Yeats inserted a note to this poem in *The Wanderings of Oisin and Other Poems*, 1889: "This is an attempt to reconstruct an old song from three lines imperfectly remembered, by an old peasant woman in the village of Ballysodare, Sligo, who often sings them to herself."

"The Ballad of Father O'Hart." Yeats inserted these notes to this poem in *Fairy and Folk Tales of the Irish Peasantry*, 1888:
    "*Shoneen*—i.e., upstart.
    "*Sleiveen*—i.e., mean fellow.

"Coloony is a few miles south of the town of Sligo. Father O'Hart lived there in the last century, and was greatly beloved. These lines accurately record the tradition. No one who has held the stolen land has prospered. It has changed owners many times."

The Wanderings of Oisin—BOOK I. Oisin describes to Saint Patric his journey with the fair Niam, daughter of the King of Tin-nan-Oge, the Land of the Young, on the magic white horse. They live in the Island of the Living for a hundred years, but one day Oisin finds by the sea the staff of a dead warrior and remembers his companions of the Fianna. They depart on their magic horse. BOOK II. They reach the Island of Victories, where they discover a maiden who is the prisoner of a demon. Oisin fights the demon for another hundred years. He then again remembers the Fianna, and he and Niam depart for the Island of Forgetfulness. BOOK III. The lovers sleep amidst the heroes of Ireland until Oisin is awakened by the fall of a starling, and again he makes for the Fianna. He says farewell to Niam and departs on the magic horse. Niam warns him not to touch the earth with any part of his body. He finds none of his companions in Ireland, but on his way back to Niam he leans from his saddle to help two men lift a sack of sand and the girths break. As he falls to earth his years descend upon him and he becomes a frail old man. He is brought to Patric, who warns him of the flames of hell. Oisin, whose age has not dimmed his spirit, declares that he prefers to remain with the Fenians for eternity.

There are many variant spellings of the proper names. For instance, in later editions—and in other poems—Yeats changed Niam to Niamh, Maive to Maeve, Patric to Patrick, and Oisin to Usheen.

"To the Rose upon the Rood of Time." Yeats explained in later years that the quality symbolized by the Rose differs from the Intellectual Beauty of Shelley and of Spenser in that he imagined it as suffering with man and not as something pursued from afar. The Rose poems were written for Maud Gonne, but also partake of his chaotic ideas taken from many sources. The Rose, incidentally, is a favourite symbol in Irish poetry, both in Gaelic and in English.

"Fergus and the Druid." The Celtic subject-matter in this poem gives Yeats an opportunity to praise the dreamer over the man of action. Fergus the King gives up his kingdom for poetry. The idea of reincarnation came to the poet primarily from Mohini Chatterjee, but was also a part of pagan Irish tradition.

"The Death of Cuchulain." Retitled "Cuchulain's Fight with the Sea" in *Early Poems and Stories,* 1925.

"Rosa Mundi." Retitled "The Rose of the World" in *The Countess Kathleen and Various Legends and Lyrics,* 1892. The Rose poems in this book were strongly influenced by the poets of the nineties whom he met at the Rhymers' Club, especially Lionel Johnson, to whom he dedicated them.

"The Man Who Dreamed of Faeryland." This important poem, in addition to expressing the young poet's aloofness and his longing for "the twilight companies" of dreams, is directly autobiographical in the lines
> He wandered by the sands of Lisadill;
> His mind ran all on money cares and fears . . .
In the summer months, when his money ran low, he always returned to Sligo, where he could live with relatives.

"The Lamentation of the Old Pensioner." "A Visionary" in *The Celtic Twilight* gives a full account of the source of this poem. The old visionary, who repeats again and again "the fret [Irish for doom] is over me," reminds Yeats of his friend and former schoolmate, George Russell, or AE, the mystic, poet, and economist.

"The Ballad of Father Gilligan." According to the poet, the source of this poem is a tradition among the people of Castleisland, Kerry.

"The Two Trees." This poem draws its images from Yeats's

studies in Blake and the cabala. The cabala unfolds the "way" leading from the human heart, through the "Sephiroth" or archetypal ideas, to union with the divine. The Sephirotic tree, however, presents two faces to the world—one benign, the other malign. The poet completes his song with imagery suggestive of the Yggdrasil of Norse myth, where, like Cuchulain in his dance-play, Odin comes in search of wisdom with his ravens and purchases it at the cost of an eye. F. A. C. Wilson notes that this poem is the first statement of Yeats's theory of subjectivity and objectivity (F. A. C. Wilson, *Yeats's Iconography,* London: 1960, pp. 251-254).

"To Ireland in the Coming Times." The poem is the epilogue to the volume of *The Rose.* It was written in self-defence against the poet's friends O'Leary, Maud Gonne, and the other fanatical young Irelanders who had criticized the esoteric Rose poems.

"The Moods." This exquisite little poem expresses an idea that reappears in some of the stronger poems of Yeats's old age, such as "Supernatural Songs," written in 1934.

"The Stolen Bride." Retitled "The Host of the Air" in *The Wind Among the Reeds,* 1899. It was first published in *The Bookman,* November, 1893, where Yeats included this note after the title: "I heard the story on which this ballad is founded from an old woman at Balesodare, Sligo. She repeated me a Gaelic poem on the subject, and then translated it to me. I have always regretted not having taken down her words, and as some amends for not having done so, have made this ballad. Any one who tastes fairy food or drink is glamoured and stolen by the fairies. This is why Bridget sets O'Driscoll to play cards. 'The folk of the air' is a Gaelic name for the fairies."

"Mongan laments the Change . . ." Retitled "He mourns for the change that has come upon him and his Beloved, and longs for the End of the World" in *Lyrical Poems,* 1906. This is like a Celtic riddle-poem. It is autobiographical and records the poet's despair when he discovers that his relations with Diana Vernon, instead of tranquillizing his worship of Maud Gonne, had transformed it into a remorseless craving for possession. The symbolism reappears in *Oisin*. The boar without bristles refers to the beast that slew Attis, Adonis, and Diarmuid, and symbolizes darkness and doom. The poem recalls the pagan "Song of Amergin," who describes his transformations. Yeats knew from Jubainville that the practitioners of Druidic "science" learned to identify themselves with everything that lives, and thus to become equal with the gods.

"Cap and Bell." Retitled "The Cap and Bells" in *The Second Book of the Rhymers' Club,* 1894. This ghostly poem records a dream to which he refers in his *Autobiographies*. In his despair, Yeats was absorbing himself more and more in the occult, and his mentor, MacGregor Mathers, warned him that he was lost in the life of a chameleon.

"The Valley of the Black Pig." The initial publication of this poem was in *The Savoy* for April, 1896. Yeats included this note after the title:

"The Irish peasantry have for generations comforted themselves, in their misfortunes, with visions of a great battle, to be fought in a mysterious valley called, 'The Valley of the Black Pig,' and to break at last the power of their enemies. A few years ago, in the barony of Lisadell, in county Sligo, an old man would fall entranced upon the ground from time to time, and rave out a description of the battle; and I have myself heard said that the girths shall rot from the bellies of the horses, because of the few men that shall come alive out of the valley."

"The Twilight of Forgiveness." Retitled "The Lover asks Forgiveness because of his Many Moods" in *Lyrical Poems,* 1906.

"The Valley of Lovers." Retitled "He tells of a Valley full of Lovers" in *Lyrical Poems,* 1906.

"Poem by O'Sullivan the Red Concerning Mary Lavell I." Retitled "He tells of the Perfect Beauty" in *Lyrical Poems,* 1906. Yeats changed his poetical style in 1896, and began to write poems describing the passions of individuals called O'Sullivan Rua, Michael Robartes, Aedh, Hanrahan, and Mongan. The poet described them in detail in the notes he added to *The Wind Among the Reeds,* 1899. He has used these individuals, he says, as principles of the mind rather than as active personages. According to magical tradition, "Michael Robartes" is fire reflected in water; Hanrahan is fire blown by the wind; Aedh, whose name is not merely the Irish form of Hugh, but the Irish for fire, is fire burning by itself. Hanrahan, to put it in a different way, is the simplicity of an imagination too changeable to gather permanent possessions, or the adoration of the shepherd; Michael Robartes is the pride of the imagination brooding upon the greatness of the possessions, or the adoration of the Magi; Aedh is the myrrh and frankincense that the imagination offers continually before all that it loves. Yeats intended these characters to be shadowy projections of his personality.

"O'Sullivan the Red upon his Wanderings." Retitled "Maid Quiet" in *Poems: Second Series,* 1909. This poem was first published in *The National Observer,* December 24, 1892, where Yeats added the following note after the title: " 'Gulleon's place of pride' is the mountain now called 'The Fews,' and once called 'Sleive Fua.' It is fabled to be his (Hanrahan's) tomb, and was doubtless the place of his worship, for Gulleon was Cullain, a god of the underworld. The 'pale deer' were certain deer, hunted once by Cuchulain in his battle fury, and, as I understand them, symbols of night and shadow."

"The Travail of Passion." This is one of the poems written in the disturbed year 1896, and addressed to Diana Vernon. These poems are in contrast to those written before by their increased awareness of physical passion.

"Aedh Wishes His Beloved Were Dead." In later versions of these poems "Aedh" has been changed to "He."

"Aedh Wishes for the Cloths of Heaven." According to F. A. C. Wilson this is the poet's most consummate early lyric. Aedh symbolizes Yeats as the dreamy, defeated lover (F. A. C. Wilson, *op. cit,* p. 247).

"In the Seven Woods." This was written of the Coronation festivities of Edward VII, in 1902. During this time the poet retreated to the seven woods of Coole Park, Lady Gregory's demesne in the West.

"Untitled Song." Titled "Red Hanrahan's Song about Ireland" in *Lyrical Poems,* 1906.

SOURCES OF THE POEMS

Miserrimus   *Dublin University Review,* October, 1886
Voices   *Dublin University Review,* March, 1885
The Indian upon God   *Poems.* Boston: 1895
The Indian to His Love   *Poems.* London: 1901
The Stolen Child   *Irish Monthly,* December, 1886
To an Isle in the Water   *Poems.* Boston: 1895
Down by the Salley Gardens   *Poems.* Boston: 1895
The Meditation of the Old Fisherman   *Poems.* Boston: 1895
The Ballad of Father O'Hart   *Poems.* Boston: 1895
The Ballad of Moll Magee   *Poems.* Boston: 1895
The Wanderings of Oisin   *Poems.* London: 1901
To the Rose upon the Rood of Time   *Poems.* London: 1901
Fergus and the Druid   *National Observer,* May 21, 1892
The Death of Cuchulain   *Poems.* London: 1901
Rosa Mundi   *National Observer,* January 2, 1892
The Rose of Peace   *Poems.* London: 1901
The Rose of Battle   *Poems.* London: 1901
A Fairy Song   *National Observer,* September 12, 1891
The Lake Isle of Innisfree   *Poems.* Boston: 1895
The Pity of Love   *Poems.* Boston: 1895
The Sorrow of Love   *Poems.* Boston: 1895
When You Are Old   *Poems.* London: 1901
The White Birds   *Poems.* Boston: 1895
A Dream of Death   *Poems.* Boston: 1895
The Man who Dreamed of Faeryland   *Poems.* Boston: 1895

The Lamentation of the Old Pensioner   *Poems.* Boston: 1895

The Ballad of Father Gilligan   *Poems.* London: 1901

The Two Trees   *Poems.* Boston: 1895

To Ireland in the Coming Times   *Poems.* Boston: 1895

The Everlasting Voices   *The Wind Among the Reeds.* New York: 1899

The Moods   *The Wind Among the Reeds.* New York: 1899

The Stolen Bride   *The Bookman,* November, 1893

The Song of Wandering Aengus   *The Wind Among the Reeds.* New York: 1899

The Fiddler of Dooney   *The Wind Among the Reeds.* New York: 1899

Mongan laments the Change that has come upon him and his Beloved   *The Wind Among the Reeds.* New York: 1899

O'Sullivan Rua to Mary Lavell   *The Savoy,* July, 1896

Aedh gives his Beloved Certain Rhymes   *The Wind Among the Reeds.* New York: 1899

Cap and Bell   *National Observer,* March 17, 1894

The Valley of the Black Pig   *The Wind Among the Reeds.* New York: 1899

The Twilight of Forgiveness   *The Saturday Review,* November 2, 1895

The Valley of Lovers   *The Saturday Review,* January 9, 1897

Poem by O'Sullivan the Red Concerning Mary Lavell I   *United Ireland,* April 11, 1896

The Secret Rose   *The Wind Among the Reeds.* New York: 1899

O'Sullivan the Red upon his Wanderings   *New Review,* August, 1897

The Travail of Passion   *The Savoy,* January, 1896

Hanrahan speaks to the Lovers of his Songs in Coming Days   *The Wind Among the Reeds.* New York: 1899

Aedh wishes his Beloved Were Dead   *The Wind Among the Reeds.* New York: 1899

Aedh wishes for the Cloths of Heaven   *The Wind Among the Reeds.* New York: 1899

In the Seven Woods   *In the Seven Woods.* New York:
    1903
The Arrow   *In the Seven Woods.* New York: 1903
Old Memory   *Wayfarer's Love.* London: 1904
Untitled Song   *A Broad Sheet,* April, 1903
The Players ask for a Blessing on the Psalteries and Them-
    selves   *In the Seven Woods.* New York: 1903
The Old Age of Queen Maeve   *The Fortnightly Review.*
    April, 1903

OTHER WORKS BY
WILLIAM BUTLER YEATS

The Countess Kathleen, 1892   Play

The Land of Heart's Desire, 1894   Play

The Pot of Broth, 1902   Play

Cathleen ni Houlihan, 1902   Play

The King's Threshold, 1903   Play

Ideas of Good and Evil, 1903   Essays

The Hour Glass, 1903   Play

On Baile's Strand, 1904   Play

Deirdre, 1906   Play

Reveries Over Childhood and Youth, 1915 Autobiography

The Wild Swans at Coole, 1917   Poems

The Trembling of the Veil, 1922   Autobiography

SELECTED BIBLIOGRAPHY
AND CRITICISM

Ellmann, Richard. *The Identity of Yeats.* New York: Oxford University Press; London: Macmillan & Company, Ltd., 1954.

Hall, James and Steinmann, Martin (eds.). *The Permanence of Yeats.* New York: The Macmillan Company, 1950.

Henn, Thomas Rice. *The Lonely Tower: Studies in the Poetry of W. B. Yeats.* London: Methuen & Company, Ltd., 1950; New York: Pellegrini & Cudahy, 1952.

Hoare, D. M. *The Works of Morris and of Yeats in Relation to Early Saga Literature.* New York: The Macmillan Company; London: Cambridge University Press, 1937.

Hone, Joseph. *W. B. Yeats, 1865–1939.* New York and London: The Macmillan Company, 1937.

Jeffares, A. N. *W. B. Yeats: The Man and Poet.* New Haven, Conn.: Yale University Press; London: Routledge & Kegan Paul, Ltd., 1949.

Menon, V. K. N. *The Development of William Butler Yeats.* London: Oliver & Boyd, Ltd., 1960; Chester Springs, Pa.: Dufour Editions, 1961.

Moore, Virginia. *The Unicorn: William Butler Yeats' Search for Reality.* New York: The Macmillan Company, 1954.

Rudd, Margaret. *Divided Image: A Study of William Blake and W. B. Yeats.* London: Routledge & Kegan Paul, Ltd., 1953.

Seiden, Morton I. *William Butler Yeats: The Poet as Mythmaker.* East Lansing, Mich.: Michigan State University Press, 1961.

Stock, Amy G. *W. B. Yeats: His Poetry and Thought.* London: Cambridge University Press, 1961.

Unterecker, John. *The Reader's Guide to William Butler Yeats.* The Noonday Press, 1959.

Ussher, Arland. *Three Great Irishmen: Shaw, Yeats, Joyce.* London: Victor Gollancz, Ltd.; New York: New American Library (Mentor Books) 1957.

Wade, Allan (ed.). *The Letters of W. B. Yeats.* New York: The Macmillan Company; London: Rupert Hart-Davis, Ltd., 1954.

Winters, Ivor. *The Poetry of W. B. Yeats.* Denver, Col.: Alan Swallow, Publisher, 1960.

Outstanding SIGNET CLASSICS

THE INFORMER *by Liam O'Flaherty*

This story of a hunted man who has betrayed his friend to the enemy presents a harshly realistic picture of Ireland divided by the Civil War in the 1920's. Afterword by Donagh McDonagh.
(#CP80—60¢)

PLAYS *by George Bernard Shaw*

Arms and the Man, Candida, Man and Superman, and Mrs. Warren's Profession. Introduction by Eric Bentley.
(#CP118—60¢)

ADVENTURES IN THE SKIN TRADE and Other Stories
by Dylan Thomas

Brilliant and fantastic tales by the great Welsh poet, who writes of sinners and lovers, nature and madness. Afterword by Vernon Watkins.
(#CD38—50¢)

LEAVES OF GRASS *by Walt Whitman*

Whitman's enduring testament to a land whose vitality was the touchstone of his genius. A complete edition. Introduction by Gay Wilson Allen, the Whitman authority.
(#CT23—75¢)

ALICE'S ADVENTURES IN WONDERLAND and THROUGH THE LOOKING GLASS *by Lewis Carroll*

The immortal classic of a little girl who enters fantasy land via a rabbit hole. Foreword by Horace Gregory. With the original Tenniel illustrations.
(#CD22—50¢)

THE PICTURE OF DORIAN GRAY and Selected Stories
by Oscar Wilde

The title story plus "Lord Arthur Sevile's Crime," and two fairy tales, "The Happy Prince" and "The Birthday of the Infanta." Foreword by Gerald Weales.
(#CP115—60¢)

ATALA and RENE *by Francois René de Chateaubriand*

Two charming romantic tales, whose heroes are American Indians, by the French author who has been called "the true founder of Romanticism in France." Newly translated, with a Foreword by Walter J. Cobb.
(#CD103—50¢)

IDYLLS OF THE KING and a Selection of Poems
by Alfred Lord Tennyson

The Arthurian romance and other poetry by the famous Victorian bard. Foreword by George Barker.
(#CD42—50¢)

More Outstanding SIGNET CLASSICS

TO OUR READERS: We welcome your request for our free catalog of
SIGNET and MENTOR books. If your dealer does not have the books
you want, you may order them by mail, enclosing the list price
plus 5¢ a copy to cover mailing. The New American Library of
World Literature, Inc., P.O. Box 2310, Grand Central Station,
New York 17, N. Y.